BETRAYED

Book Three in the Forbidden Series

by Melody Anne

COPYRIGHT

DEDICATION

This book is dedicated to Sage. Thank you for making my dad's life so much better. You bring him joy and happiness. You're a loving, wonderful person, and I'm glad to know you and love you.

BOOKS BY MELODY ANNE

BILLIONAIRE BACHELORS

*The Billionaire Wins the Game

*The Billionaire's Dance

*The Billionaire Falls

*The Billionaire's Marriage Proposal

*Blackmailing the Billionaire

*Runaway Heiress

*The Billionaire's Final Stand

*Unexpected Treasure

*Hidden Treasure

*Holiday Treasure

BABY FOR THE BILLIONAIRE

+The Tycoon's Revenge

+The Tycoon's Vacation

+The Tycoon's Proposal

+The Tycoon's Secret

+The Lost Tycoon

RISE OF THE DARK ANGEL

-Midnight Fire – Rise of the Dark Angel – Book One

-Midnight Moon – Rise of the Dark Angel – Book Two

-Midnight Storm – Rise of the Dark Angel – Book Three

-Midnight Eclipse – Rise of the Dark Angel – Book Four – **Coming Soon**

SURRENDER

=Surrender – Book One

=Submit – Book Two

=Seduced – Book Three

=Scorched – Book Four

FORBIDDEN SERIES

+Bound – Book One

+Broken – Book Two

+Betrayed – Book Three

+Burned – Book Four – Coming March 2015

UNEXPECTED HEROES SERIES

-Safe in His Arms – Novella – *Baby, It's Cold Outside* Anthology

-Her Unexpected Hero – Book One – **Releases Feb 28th 2015**

-Who I Am with You – Novella – **Releases April 27th 2015**

-Her Hometown Hero – Book Two – **Releases June 30th 2015**

-Following Her – Novella – **Releases Sept 14th 2015**

-Her Forever Hero – **Releases Feb 2016**

TAKEN BY A TRILLIONAIRE SERIES

-*Ruth Cardello, Melody Anne, and J.S. Scott* – **Releases May 2015**

PROLOGUE

MCKENZIE FLIPPED OFF her blankets with an angry shove, thrust her feet into her slippers, and blindly reached for her robe. Then she stomped through her house until she made it to the front door. The loud pounding continued unabated. It was what had woken her up and put her in such a terrible mood.

"Go away!" she shouted through the door. She didn't give a damn who was knocking. It was two in the morning, and she wasn't about to invite the ill-mannered person in.

"I'm not leaving until we talk!" a man shouted right back at her.

She froze, suddenly almost overcome by fear. But no. She was McKenzie Beaumont, dammit, and she didn't frighten easily.

"I'm calling the police," she growled.

"Fine with me. The chief is a personal friend," he said with just enough arrogance that he might be telling the truth.

"Who are you?" she asked, her voice much less angry. Despite her bravado, the fear had returned in spades, and a shiver ran down her spine.

"Byron Knight!" he shouted back.

"Byron?" She opened the small window that would show her who was standing on her doorstep. She was shocked to see that it *was* Byron, Blake Knight's brother. "What in the world are you doing on my doorstep at this time of morning?" she asked.

Then she started to panic. What if something had happened to Blake? Or to Jewell? Without thinking, she unlocked the door and thrust it open. "What's wrong? What's going on?"

Though she'd seen the man only a few times before, he took her open door as an invitation and walked right inside.

"What's wrong?" she asked again.

"I have a question for you, Ms. Beaumont," he said, and that's when she smelled the alcohol on his breath and noticed the narrowed eyes.

She never should have opened her door. She knew Blake, but that didn't mean she knew his brother.

"Just ask your question and then get the hell out of my house," she said, thrusting her shoulders back as she got ready to do battle. She had been to hell and back more than once. There was no way this man was going to intimidate her.

"Just who do you think you are?" he said menacingly.

"I'm sorry, Byron, but you're going to have to be a little bit more specific than that," she said, placing her hands on her hips.

"You think you can mess with people's lives and get

away with it. Well, I'm here to prove you wrong."

McKenzie stumbled back a step when he started stalking her, and then she was up against a wall with his arms caging her in.

"If you touch me, I'll press charges," she warned him.

"Oh, McKenzie, you will soon learn I'm not one of the timid little men you're used to dealing with."

And then he lowered his head to meet hers.

CHAPTER ONE

Three Months Later

MCKENZIE LOCKED THE front door for the last time and took a deep breath. She wasn't a weak woman or prone to tears — not ever — and closing this door meant opening another one. But … She was still walking away from a building and a career that had changed her life.

For the better.

Most people would say that career had been immoral, had enslaved women, and catered to the whims of the worst sort of men. She had to disagree. McKenzie had been on the wrong side of a sick man's lust once, and she'd built her business on saving women, not enslaving them.

Her deep desire to rebuild herself had consumed her for years after what her first love had done to her. It was hard to shake the trauma of that time in her life. But…no. She shook her head to clear away the horrid thoughts of her past. She wouldn't go there, wouldn't think of those awful days, those days when she hadn't been able to look in a mirror for fear of what she would see looking back at her.

Everyone thought she was experienced, a woman of the world, and that's what she wanted them to see. Cool, calm, and collected, untouched by anything. But she'd truly been to hell and back. More importantly, she was still surviving the ride she'd been on for fifteen years. And now a new chapter in her life was opening.

She'd said her goodbye's last week, and a part of her would mourn for a long time to come, but a part of her was now free. She tried to suppress the guilt that thought brought to her, but it had been fifteen years, and it was time to let go.

"It's been a pleasure doing business with you, McKenzie. What's your next adventure?"

McKenzie turned to look at the real estate agent who had helped her sell the building. She was a nice woman in her early thirties, a woman who'd never had a hard day in her life. But then again, how did McKenzie know that? Just because the woman wore a pale blue suit and a small silver barrette in her hair, that didn't mean she was as nice or as happy or as innocent as she looked. She could have a drawer — or a toybox — full of whips and chains in her apartment, and her fantasies could be of tying men up like dogs and making them bark.

Everyone had secrets. It was only a matter of time before others discovered them.

"With the profit I've made from this sale, I'll be able to complete setting up the accounting firm I've been wanting to open for the past three years, since I finished my degree," McKenzie replied.

Shirley laughed. "Accounting, huh? I wouldn't have taken you for the type to sit behind a desk and pore over numbers all day long. As busy as you always are, how did you manage to complete a degree?"

Nosy woman, McKenzie thought, but that's not what she said. "I started by taking night classes, then when my work here was more busy in the evening, I took classes at the community college in the day. It took some extra time, but I discovered I have a real knack for numbers."

"Well, I say that you're far too beautiful to hide in a windowless room," the agent said with another laugh.

"Ah, but looks can be deceiving," McKenzie told her with a wink. "And trust me, I will have plenty of windows. I like the freedom of opening them and feeling a breeze, even in this rainy area." She handed the woman the keys and turned to lead them both to the parking area behind the building.

"Yes, looks aren't always what they appear," Shirley said.

That laugh again. It was delicate but oddly pointed. McKenzie began to think she might be right about Shirley. Not so innocent at all.

The two women made it to their cars, shook hands, and parted ways. As McKenzie drove off, she knew she wouldn't have contact with Shirley again. She wasn't a girl-bonding kind of gal. As a matter of fact, the only woman she'd become close to since she was a teenager was Jewell Weston. Or Jewell Knight, to use her new name.

It had taken McKenzie a while, but she'd now admit that Jewell was a friend. Most certainly. And she smiled at the thought, but her lips quickly turned down into a frown. When she'd met Jewell in that cold, rat-infested building last year, McKenzie had thought she'd been saving the young woman.

Had she known at the time that Jewell was so innocent — a virgin in fact, and an idealistic one — she never would have brought her to Relinquish Control. Luckily, it had all turned out well, for Jewell at least, since she was now married to a wonderful man — well, a recently changed and now wonderful man. Plus, Jewell was now three months pregnant, and McKenzie had never seen her happier.

Not only didn't McKenzie get into girl bonding in the usual way, but she'd never been a baby type of gal, either. She'd never wanted to hold them, had never felt her biological clock ticking, and had never wanted a white picket fence, kids, pets, and the whole American Dream. Some said that made her abnormal. She chose to believe that it made her focused on what really mattered.

But she couldn't deny that she was excited at the thought of meeting Jewell and Blake's first child. He or she was surely going to be as beautiful as the two of them were. McKenzie had even found herself shopping with Jewell for baby clothes the week before.

They had run into Byron.

That memory sent a shudder through her just as she pulled up to a red light. She hit her brake pedal a little too hard, locking her seatbelt against her and making her unable to move for a moment.

"Byron Knight," she growled.

That man had been running through her brain constantly for the past three months — hell, he'd taken up shop there — ever since the night he'd shown up at her door, accused her of ruining his brother's life, kissed her senseless, and then disappeared as quickly as he'd come in.

She'd been furious when the whole disaster began, and she'd even lifted up her phone to call the police. When he started kissing her, her first impulse was to claw his eyes out. Then, after a few seconds, she'd melted against him. When he pulled back, the cocky look in his eyes — the arrogant bastard! — had made her claws come out again. But before she could strike, he was gone.

She hadn't seen him again until last week, and the look in his eyes when their gazes collided had sent strange sensations traveling up and down her spine. Absurd. Why was this man even a blip on her radar, let alone at the controls of what she felt? And what were these feelings?

No, she wasn't a fool. She knew that people enjoyed sex. Some of her "ladies" had even told her that they didn't always have to fake their orgasms when they were on the job. But for McKenzie, her one and only sexual partner had been…horrific. She shuddered even thinking about it.

But why was she thinking of Byron Knight and sex in the same sentence? Just because his kiss had heated her blood didn't mean a thing. She'd been around overconfident men for years, and they did nothing for her.

Byron Knight made no difference in her life, and he never would. Though she might be a friend of the intolerable man's sister-in-law, McKenzie would run into him only rarely. Certainly not at her new accounting business, which would open its doors on Monday.

He wouldn't know where those offices were, and a man in his income range would have no need for an accountant like her. Big boys like him swam in another pool altogether. With any luck she'd never see him again. So what if she was attracted to the man — where had that come from? She hated herself for feeling that way.

Out of sight, out of mind. That was her philosophy. If she didn't see him, didn't think about him, didn't talk about him, then she would soon forget about him. It wasn't as if he were hanging out with Jewell — he rarely showed up at Jewell and Blake's place. So McKenzie was just fine.

The stoplight changed to green — finally — and she made it to her street, pulled into the driveway, and walked inside her home. It didn't matter how many times she shut and locked her front door. When she turned and looked at her modest living room, peace washed through her.

It was her house, a house that she'd paid for completely. No bank could come and take it away like they had her mother's home.

Yes, McKenzie's life had been difficult, but the baptism by fire — okay, baptisms in the plural — had made her stronger. She was who she was because nothing had been handed to her. She was strong and independent and there wasn't anything she couldn't do.

It was time to put the finishing touches on her business plan. Next week, her life would change forever.

CHAPTER TWO

I THINK WE'RE officially in the black."

McKenzie took a break from staring at her computer screen and looked up at the smiling face of her business partner, Zach Sinclair. It really was too bad that she wasn't attracted to the man. He was intelligent — one of the most intelligent men she knew, actually — and he could make her laugh. On top of that, he was single.

Didn't matter. She felt nothing but friendship for the fellow. Maybe she was broken. She was twenty-nine years old, hadn't been in a serious relationship for ten years, and hadn't been interested in being in one, either.

There were plenty of men who had asked her out, but she turned them away. Her ex, whose very name still turned her stomach, had left quite a mark on her. She didn't need a psychoanalyst to tell her that, and knowing when and how she'd been messed up couldn't change how she felt.

Oh, yes. They were in the black. "Did you ever doubt we would be?" she asked.

"No. But most businesses don't make a profit in the first two months. It usually takes years," he replied as he propped himself on the edge of her desk. Their doors had been open officially for two months this coming Friday, and business was good — or better than she had pictured at this point.

"That's why we save for the rainy days, Zach. But we still bust our asses so we don't have to rely on those savings."

"Well, don't get too excited, sweetheart. We're only in the black by a very small margin. We need to land more clients pronto."

"We're new. It will take time for big clients to trust us, and to feel that we are not only competent, but *better* than all the other accounting firms. Until then, we have a lot to smile about, though, because we already have ten full-time employees and six part-timers. We're doing better than most."

"Yes, that's true. And I have meetings with potential clients every day this week."

"I was afraid to take on a partner, Zach — you know that. But you've given me reason to hope that some of you men are actually worth trusting."

"Ah, coming from you, that's a real compliment," he replied. "And we meshed well when I was your teacher in college. I knew three years ago that you were going places. I'm glad you took me up on the offer to open this place. We're going to be the finest accounting firm in all of Seattle."

He'd impressed her with his teaching skills, and he still taught a night class two days a week, but to have his own business had been Zach's dream. If she hadn't been in several of his classes over a three-year stretch, she never would have had the confidence in him to go into business together. But she'd watched him do his job well, and then she'd shared a few coffees with him during his office hours when she came by to ask questions. It really was too bad she didn't feel an attraction for him. But it was great that he'd never shown one for her.

He was thirty-five, though he acted younger than she did on most days, and he had slightly wavy blond hair and green eyes. Most women would find him charming. She found him brilliant.

The phone rang, and it rang again.

"Beth is out to lunch. You're going to have to take that," he told her, and she picked up the phone.

"Seattle Accounting, McKenzie Beaumont speaking. How may I help you?"

"Hello, Ms. Beaumont. Dixie Pedmore here. I'm calling on behalf of someone who would like to meet with you today, if possible."

McKenzie looked down at her calendar, and today wasn't the best day, but she didn't want to turn down a potential client. Still, it was good to show people that she wasn't available at the drop of a hat, that she and her time were in demand.

"I'm all booked up today, Ms. Pedmore. Could we do Friday instead?" she asked. Friday was only three days away.

The woman paused for a pregnant moment; she clearly wasn't used to people who didn't accommodate her requests. McKenzie had a way of reading people, even over the phone. When she hadn't immediately agreed, Dixie had sucked in her breath, not loudly, but just enough for McKenzie to hear it through the phone line. This piqued

McKenzie's curiosity. Who did Ms. Pedmore work for? The woman hadn't said.

"Hold for one moment, and I'll see if that will be workable," Dixie told her, quickly recovering, and before McKenzie could agree or disagree, the woman placed her on hold.

"Who is it?" Zach whispered.

McKenzie held her hand over the mouthpiece in case Dixie jumped back on the line. "I don't know," she replied. "Someone's secretary, I'm assuming."

A couple of minutes passed and then McKenzie heard the phone click as the woman came back on the line.

"Thank you for holding, Ms. Beaumont. My boss said Friday would be fine. Meet him at noon on Friday at Cutters on the Pier."

"Can I get your boss's name?" McKenzie asked, but the question got her nowhere. The woman had said what she needed to say and had hung up without even asking whether noon would be an acceptable time.

"So what's it all about?" Zach asked. "Who's the potential client?"

"I don't know. The woman hung up. No contact number, no information. Nothing." McKenzie shook her head in frustration.

"Don't go if you're worried about it," Zach said, a frown marring his normally cheerful face.

"You know that's not going to happen. I want this business to be a success, which means that I'll meet with anyone and everyone," she replied, and she took a few seconds to mark the appointment down.

"Want me to go instead?" he asked her.

"I thought you had meetings all week."

"I do," he said, the frown still in place. "But I can try to adjust my schedule."

"It's at Cutters, and I love the food there. And I promise you that I'll be fine, Zach. I've dealt with a lot of less than pleasant clients before. I'm not worried about a business lunch at a public place," she told him.

"But don't they have private meeting rooms there?"

"Yes, they do, but they're usually for larger parties. Even if I end up alone with the mystery person in one of those rooms, it wouldn't matter because of the waitstaff."

"I don't like it, but I'll trust you to do what you feel is right," Zach said before looking at his watch and grimacing. "I have to run, doll. We'll have more time to talk about this later — *before* you go or don't go."

She barely had time to tell him goodbye before he was rushing out the door. That was their lives right now. Fourteen-hour workdays followed by more work at home, and no days off. In the end it would be all worth it, though, because she would retire early, and most of the time it didn't really feel like work anyway. She truly loved her business.

Well, she loved it at least eighty percent of the time. Still, it was different from working at Relinquish Control. She couldn't say she had been unhappy owning her escort service — she had enjoyed her time there, for the most part. But there had been too many girls who had been just like her, lost, afraid, alone. It had begun to really get to her.

In this new business, she rarely even caught a glimpse of the people she managed. A client came in to request an accountant for their business, and she dispatched one. Some of the jobs turned into permanent positions, and some were temporary. Some were complicated and some easy. She was good at finding new clients, and excellent at matching up employees to businesses. Time would only make her and Zach's business that much more reputable. This was going to be her year to shine.

Pushing the unusual phone call from her mind, McKenzie looked back down at her computer, and she was immediately immersed in her work. Friday would come soon enough. She had enough to worry about without obsessing over an enigmatic phone call.

CHAPTER THREE

RIGHT THIS WAY, Ms. Beaumont."

The host was dressed impeccably, and why shouldn't he be dressed that way here, in a nice restaurant located next to the historic Pike Place Market? When they bypassed the regular dining room, McKenzie's stomach clenched just the slightest bit.

She knew this potential client had money. Or if she hadn't known it, she knew it now. It wasn't cheap or easy to get a last-minute private dining room anywhere in Seattle, let alone one with a view Elliott Bay, Mount Rainer, the Olympic Mountains, and the Port of Seattle — all in one.

Why would anyone with this kind of money be interested in her fledgling accounting firm? Who in the hell could the person be? The room she stepped into was large, but it had only one small table set up by the impressive windows looking onto the bay, and she knew right then that she *had* to have whoever it was for a client. This man — or woman — could bring her business out into the open.

"I'll hang your coat for you," the host said.

Excitement teamed up with nerves as he pulled out her chair and waited for her to hand over her coat and sit down. That accomplished, McKenzie wondered how long she would have to wait to meet this mystery person.

He — had to be a male — most likely knew that she would wait all day if that were what it took. She couldn't believe she'd gotten away with putting the person off for three days. It had been a silly power play, and it could have cost her a big client. She'd have to be more careful in the future. Would she have to do some serious sucking up now?

"Might I offer you a drink while you wait?"

"Yes, an iced tea, please," McKenzie replied.

The man vanished right away, zipped back in, and vanished again, leaving her alone in the room. This level of service was new to her. She'd made a lot of money over the years as the proprietor of a seriously upscale escort service, but the host's behavior made it clear that the person she was about to meet had a whole new level of wealth, a wealth that only a few possessed. And though she'd made a lot of money, she'd had a lot of expenses. Luxurious meals weren't one of them.

A few minutes later McKenzie knew she was no longer by herself. Her body tensed, and she had a feeling she wasn't going to be happy when she looked up, but even knowing this, she had to find out who was draining the oxygen from the room.

And there walking toward her was none other than Byron Knight. She should have known, and maybe she even had known somewhere deep down inside, but she'd refused to even think he could be the man behind that phone call. Why? Because then she wouldn't have come, and she desperately wanted this client's business. Call it her competitive nature, or her will to survive, but all she knew for sure was that she had to make it in Seattle's business world — in a business not involving sex — and Byron Knight had a lot of wealth that she wanted a piece of.

"I see you found the restaurant all right," Byron said as he walked up beside her, pausing before he moved to the place across from her and sat down.

When his knees brushed hers under the table, she cursed the intimate setting and scooted back a couple of inches. Sure, it would make eating a bit more difficult, but if she were touching him during the entire meal, she wouldn't be able to eat anything anyway.

She didn't bother to respond to his remark about finding the place. It was in downtown Seattle. Even a tourist could find the restaurant. So she cut to the chase. "Why all the secrecy, Byron?"

He smiled before answering her question with one his own. "Would you have come had you known it was me?"

McKenzie lifted her glass and took a sip before looking him in the eyes. Never show weakness, she said to herself, and she made sure she had on her most businesslike mask. She rarely wore any other one, but she found herself struggling a bit this time. "Of course I would have," she finally told him.

"Very good, McKenzie. I almost believe that."

A waiter now spoke.

"Would you like the appetizers brought out, sir?"

"Yes, please. And I'll have iced tea to drink, too," Byron said, surprising her.

"What? No alcohol at high noon?" she said, only the slightest mockery in her voice. But she hoped he remembered his boozed-up condition the last time they met.

If he did, he didn't show it. "I don't want you to accuse me of being inebriated while we have a business discussion," he fired back. "And didn't you know that the three-martini lunch went out of style before you were even born?"

"Why am I here, Byron? Are you wasting my time?" *Why not be blunt?*

The waiter set down his tea before disappearing again, presumably to grab the first course, which Byron had clearly ordered in advance.

"Not at all, McKenzie," came his easy reply. "Our head accountant has had an unfortunate accident and is out of the offices for the next thirty days — at a minimum. So I find myself in a pinch, and I've heard good things about your company."

Several plates of food appeared magically on the table, and even though McKenzie was tense, she couldn't help but appreciate the sweet aromas drifting up to her nose.

"And you want to hire us?" she asked.

"Don't be afraid to have a little — it's not as if you have to worry about calories," he said. "We might as well eat to keep up our strength."

The jerk thrust a plate toward her even though she could have easily reached it by herself. But a woman's gotta do what a woman's gotta do. She took a little of the calamari misto, some of the fried cheddar curds, and a few mussels. With so many hors d'oeuvres, she wouldn't have any room left in her stomach for anything else, but this meeting might not last long enough for her to reach the main course anyway. It all depended on what sort of game he was playing.

Byron filled a plate for himself and devoted a little time to nibbling before he spoke again. "I want to hire *you*, McKenzie."

She didn't miss the emphasis on *you*, but she chose to ignore it. Or to pretend to.

"Why don't you tell me about the project? I can tell you then if I think our company would be a good fit," she said. She was proud of herself, and of her composure. If she was bewitched, bothered, and bewildered, she knew she wasn't showing it. The story of her life.

For the next few minutes, Byron explained the needs of this branch of the family business, and McKenzie's mouth practically watered. This was the perfect sort of job. It was filled with challenges, and Knight Construction was so diversified — it had its hands in so many pieces of the corporate pie — that it wasn't just run-of-the-mill accounting work. It would take a sharp mind to cut through everything, and she had that in spades.

"Our company is more than qualified to help you," she told him. "It sounds as if these last few months have been…difficult…in some parts of the family firm."

"Not at all. But my brothers and I tend to go out to a lot of the job sites, where we can swing a hammer and get back to the basics. We do it on the assumption that we've hired a responsible enough team to do their work, and when we come back into the offices, things sometimes haven't gone as well as we'd hoped. That's why I'm stuck at the desk for a while. It doesn't help that our accountant had a boating accident. But that's what your company is there for, correct? To come in and perform when needed?"

The way he said the words, she was sure there was a double meaning, but his tone stayed level and his expression didn't change. She wanted to call him on it, but then she would look petty. Instead she sat there silently for a moment while she thought of a proper response.

"Yes, of course. We can come in when you need a temporary accountant while another goes on vacation, or we can solve problems, or we can come in more permanently. Whatever the needs are, my goal at Seattle Accounting is to ensure you will use us each time." She nearly flinched at that last line, especially when his eyes twinkled. She really needed to be a lot more careful with what she said, and how she said it.

"Well, with all the challenges of new projects, and overseas operations, our accounting team has been working nonstop. Because the head of the department has been out for the past week, it's gotten chaotic, but it's been like that for a while anyway with the turnover I mentioned in the department. I really hate to say this, but at some of our operations we're not even sure who we can trust."

I know that feeling, McKenzie said to herself.

"So I need you to start on Monday," Byron told her, "and it will be a very long week."

"I know the perfect person to send over. He's been able to solve problems that uncountable high-level clients deemed unsolvable, and he's saved their businesses and their reputations." This would be the answer! McKenzie actually felt excited about things. She would be helping behind scenes of course. There was no way she didn't want to get her hands on this.

"That won't work for me," Byron said, and he took a

bite of his salad. His voice didn't change. It was firm, but not unkind.

"I haven't even given you his résumé yet. I can fax it over right after lunch," McKenzie said. What was going on here? How could he turn down her accountant without knowing the fellow's qualifications?

"I said I want *you*, McKenzie."

She paused as she heard what he was saying. "I don't go to work sites, Byron. Of course I am involved in all operations, but I have my own business to run," she told him. "That's why I hire capable employees and place them where they're needed."

He just shrugged. "Then I guess I'll have to go somewhere else."

She paused before speaking, not wanting to sound desperate, but also not wanting to lose this job. "Why don't you just look over Jim Dallinger's dossier? I assure you, Byron, he's as qualified as I am, if not more so."

"I won't argue this point. Either I get you or there's no deal."

The waiter could probably feel the tension rolling off of her in waves as he replaced her barely touched salad with a cup of clam chowder.

"Did you order the entire meal?" she asked. She expressed enough vexation in her voice to show him she wasn't pleased, but she was always careful. She knew better than to become over-the-top rude. Always keep them guessing.

"Yes, I did," he replied, a challenge in his tone.

"Luckily, I've enjoyed the meal…so far," she said, and she took a spoonful of the soup. She'd lost her pleasure in the food, though, as her irritation levels grew.

The SOB's appetite wasn't ruined in the least. "I don't think they serve anything that's less than stellar here, McKenzie." After throwing her an annoying grin, he dug into his own chowder.

"How long are you expecting me to be the one working in your offices?" McKenzie finally asked when it was obvious he wasn't going to speak again until she did.

"Until the job is finished."

"That isn't telling me much. What if this emergency ends up going over a month? I can't leave my business that long. I could possibly fill in for a couple of weeks, maybe even a month, but there's no way I would be able to work past that," she said. If he wanted more of her time, she'd just have to turn down this job. What good would her company's reputation be if it fell apart because she was working for him and not herself?

"I think thirty days would be sufficient," he said.

It was his first compromise of the day.

"And if your current head of accounting isn't in better health by then?" she pushed. She needed him to agree to thirty days max, or she wasn't going to go along with this.

"At that time, I suppose, I'll consider having one of your employees come in."

"Is there a chance that one of my employees could come in sooner than the thirty days?"

He paused for several moments as he looked at her. "Anything is possible, McKenzie," he said before giving her a wicked smile. "If my goals have been accomplished sooner, we will discuss other employment options."

What in the hell did that mean? She wanted to shout out, *Then why not now?* But again, a tantrum wasn't going to get her anywhere.

Something in his expression really pissed her off, but she didn't want to go there. So her voice dripped honey when she said, "Thank you." If only she could attract the bees to come and sting him.

His smile widened as if he knew exactly what she was thinking. Damn him.

"Now that the initial hard work is done, I will order some wine to go with our main course," Byron said, holding up his hand. And the waiter practically appeared in a puff.

Their soup was taken away and placed before her was grilled Alaskan king salmon and a glass of fruity Pinot Noir.

With the possibility of gaining a big client but not being locked to Byron's side for an unlimited time, her appetite returned, and she thanked the waiter. It was too much of a stretch to thank Byron. She hated presumptuous men like him. Where did the guy come off thinking she wasn't intelligent enough to order her own meal? She happened to like salmon — wild salmon, of course — but what if she hadn't been a seafood fan? Did he expect her to eat the meal anyway? Most likely. That was what men like Byron Knight always expected — for a woman just to give in to what they wanted.

The two of them filled the next little while with more precise questions and answers about his accounting problems, and then it was finally time to go. Even though the meal had been fantastic, the company hadn't been exactly pleasant, and McKenzie had a whole heck of a lot to do the rest of the day and all weekend, for that matter, if she wanted to get any sleep at all while working in the Knight brothers' building instead of her own.

She really should have turned him down, but having a client like Knight Construction would look very good in her advertisements. This would mean she could hire more employees, could make a lot more money, and could build a solid reputation in Seattle for being the best of the best. She'd been working toward that goal for seven years, and this time it would be in a respectable business.

She stood up, not caring if she should have waited for Byron to stand first. She was done with business and more than done with him as company. Byron didn't take long to stand after she did. When he held up his hand again and had the waiter bring her coat over to him, she pushed back more irritation. But why was the man giving her coat to Byron instead of to her? Okay, the guy was just doing his job, so she chose not to snap at him.

"Thank you," Byron said, dismissing the man. "We're finished here."

And McKenzie was left alone with the enemy.

"I appreciate it that you came to us for your needs," McKenzie said, and she held out a hand.

"You know why I came to you, McKenzie." His tone had changed, and his eyes were burning into hers.

"Because I'm the best at my job."

She refused to play any games with this man. She considered herself worldly and experienced, but he made her feel like… Like what? Like a kitten? A little kitten with claws she didn't know how to use yet.

"Yes, and because I have unfinished business with you," Byron said.

"What unfinished business are you talking about?"

He stepped up close to her, his lips a firm line. He didn't touch her, but he didn't need to. This man commanded a room no matter where he was or who he was with — just as he was commanding her feet to stay firmly planted right there where they were.

She didn't like it one little bit.

"You messed with my family," he said. "Now it's my turn to figure you out and find out if you have an ulterior motive for screwing with Blake."

McKenzie gasped, too stunned for several moments to say a word. When she was finally able to speak, the words came out barely above a whisper. "Is this job fake?" She was finally able to take a step back.

"Not at all. If you please me in your work, I'll back off. But I want to know what makes you tick. I don't believe in lying and I'm not the easiest person to work for. So, if you can't take the heat…" He left the sentence unfinished. He moved a step closer to match every step she took back until she found herself against the windows.

"Why should I take this job? From what you've said, it's a losing battle, at least for me." She sounded angry, but she was angriest at the slightly breathless quality in her tone.

"If you're who I think you are, then, yes, you'll lose."

At least he was straightforward. But so was she.

"Then I shouldn't take the job," she said.

"The choice is yours."

She firmed her shoulders. "I don't play games, Byron," she told him. Managing to step around him and free herself from his gaze, she looked out at the picturesque view over the bay.

"Neither do I," he said. His hand came up to her shoulder and he turned her around to face him again.

Her heart was in her throat. She had no doubt that she should walk away, but the pay was great, and the reality was that she had nothing to hide, so there was no way for this man to hurt her. So, he would be the one losing this battle here, not her. If she backed down now, he would think she was up to something. Why was it that when a person looked at you as if you were guilty, it made you shift on your feet, even when you hadn't committed the crime? She'd probably never have the answer to that.

Looking him in the eye, her back straight, she made her decision.

"Then we have an understanding." Her voice was firm.

"I guess we do. Let's seal the deal."

McKenzie knew exactly how he planned on sealing the deal, and she was damned if she was going to let that happen. Stepping sideways, she managed to get away from his grasp, and after putting an appropriate distance between them, she stuck out her hand.

Byron smiled, though that smile certainly didn't show up in his eyes, and finally he reached out and took her fingers. But instead of offering a handshake like a normal person did, he held tightly to them and then he was raising her hand to his lips and placing a kiss on her palm.

"I look forward to Monday," he said, still holding her hand close to his mouth.

"You can release me now," she said, her face blank, though she refused to break eye contact.

"Are you sure you want me to?"

"You're an arrogant bastard, aren't you?" she asked sweetly, her lips turning up in a mocking smile.

His eyes widened just the slightest at her remark, and then a true smile flitted to his glorious lips, shocking her more than anything else he'd done. "That I am, Ms. Beaumont; that I am," he said.

He released her at last, and she fled the restaurant before he could say or do anything else. When she felt she was far enough away to breathe, she stopped and leaned against a wall.

What in the world had she just gotten herself into?

CHAPTER FOUR

HAD SHE RUINED the tile in her accounting firm's foyer? McKenzie had definitely given it a beating when she walked inside. She blew past her secretary and was thinking about slamming her door shut. It took all her legendary self-control to keep from doing so. Still, she got a measure of satisfaction as she took out her foul mood on her purse by tossing it into one of the empty chairs with a little extra vigor.

She stormed around her desk and sank into her seat. She leaned forward and closed her eyes, resting her forehead on her hands and taking a deep breath. She was out of sorts, to put it mildly, and more than a little frustrated. She knew she should have turned down the job, but it was too good to be true.

Which meant that it probably was going to come back and bite her in the ass — hard!

"Meeting went well, I see."

McKenzie growled before she looked up and tried to give a semblance of a smile to Zach as he perched on her desk. The guy had never even heard of knocking.

"I do have chairs, you know," she told him, but it was something she had said many times before. He didn't seem to like chairs, and that was just one of his many endearing quirks. "And how's this for another hint, Zach? I don't want to talk about the meeting."

"You know, darling, that we're going to banter back and forth for several minutes while you pretend you don't need anyone, including me, and then you'll finally cave in and tell me all about it. So why don't we just skip the routine? It won't kill you to come right to the point. Inquiring minds want to know."

She growled again. She knew he was right, but knowing he was right didn't make her want to share anything with him. But if she didn't get this off her chest, she might just go out of her mind.

She reasoned with herself that he *was* her business partner and therefore had a right to the information. It wasn't as if she were acting weak by telling him what was happening. Plus, she didn't have to fill him in on the sexual-tension part of the story. Everyone in the business world knew that the Knight brothers had a reputation for being a pain in the ass to work with. Those men thought they were gods.

"Come on, McKenzie, how did the meeting go? Who was it? Please tell me that we are going to bring in more riches than we could ever possibly spend in our lifetime."

"It was a horrible meeting," she grumbled.

"Well, we've had failed meetings before. Just because we didn't get this one client doesn't mean it's the end of the world. My meeting went well, even though it was just a mom-and-pop place. We will make this work."

Zach was ever the optimist.

"We did get the job." Why she was fighting a panic attack she didn't know. Byron was a dirtbag — a true kick-you-when-you-are-down sort of man — but he wasn't going to force her into doing anything she didn't want to do. Maybe that was the problem. She was worried that she would want to do lots of things with him. Things she most certainly would regret.

"All right, sugar britches. I'd never even try to decipher the female mind, but I have to ask you this: Why aren't you a lot happier about obtaining another client? Until now, I thought it was just small-potatoes stuff that you considered a waste of our time."

"He has demanded that I work there personally," she groused, finally making eye contact with Zach.

His jaw dropped and he was for once silent, if only for a moment. "How in the world will this place run if you're working at a job site?" he asked her. A bit of worry had crept into his usually bright eyes.

"I don't know. That's why I'm frustrated," she said, her voice rising and her hands lifting into the air. She'd barely fought back the urge to yell.

"Um…do we need this client that badly? Who in the heck is it?" Zach asked, rapidly regaining his composure.

Good for him.

"Knight Construction." She didn't need to add more. The name was powerful in itself.

Her partner was quiet as he thought over the different options. She could practically see the wheels turning. If one of the Knight brothers wanted McKenzie to work there in person, that's exactly what would happen. You just didn't turn down clients like them.

And she and Zach both knew it.

"We do have very good employees, McKenzie. Did you point that out to him?"

"*Of course* I pointed it out to him, dammit."

"I just had to ask," Zach said in self-defense.

She had to tell him something or he was going to be spinning for a while. This wasn't their typical situation. "I…uh…kind of have some personal business with him from a previous job. I guess he figures he's killing two birds with one stone." Was she giving anything away in her voice? She hoped not. She didn't want Zach to go from point A to point Z in a matter of milliseconds with his own fantastic conclusions.

"Personal…or business?" he said slowly.

McKenzie Beaumont never shared anything personal with anyone. Okay, except for maybe little tiny snippets with Jewell, but even that was rare. Zach very much knew this, so she was a bit peeved with his pushing the personal and business words she'd hurriedly put together, but she had sort of opened up that jar.

"Does it really matter?" she said with a huff. "He thinks it's personal. I don't."

"Okay, you're going to play things close to your vest. That's what you always do, but I think you should really think about this. Yes, we could use the boost we'd get from having a client as powerful as Knight Construction, but it could also kill us if this man has some private agenda against you. If he disses our business, we'll be royally screwed."

Zach was always the voice of reason, and McKenzie thought about his words for a moment before speaking. "Byron Knight is an ass of the highest order — or lowest order." *Damn. She really didn't want to be thinking about his ass.* "And though he's gunning for me, I don't think he's unethical in business. If I do the job well, which of course I will, I seriously doubt he'll slander us. My working there will bring us in a lot of money for the actual job, and then word of mouth will help our company immeasurably," she said. And she tried not to think about Byron's mouth.

"Well, then, I guess you are going to take the job," Zach said, his smile back in place.

"And I'll work nights on business here," she promised him.

"I can handle things here. You already don't sleep enough. I'll bring in a temp employee to keep up with the crap work, and you just worry about securing us a good full-time position with Knight Construction," he said, springing down from her desk.

"I can't just walk away from the work here, Zach." McKenzie felt pushed out, but that was absurd.

"You can take a break from here with daily and nightly emails and phone calls from me to assure yourself we aren't going under. This will build our business," he told her, looking more professional than she'd ever seen him. Gone was the carefree look that he wore so well.

"I don't know how I would do this without you, Zach," she said in a rare moment of open affection.

"Of course you don't, sweetie. You wouldn't survive a day without me," he told her, then surprised her when he moved around her desk, knelt in front of her, and grabbed one of her hands. "Don't let this upset you. You're McKenzie Freaking Beaumont, badass businesswoman."

She couldn't help but smile at the combination of serious tone and almost flippant words. "I really do appreciate you, Zach," she said while tugging against his hold. She didn't do well with casual touching.

Zach knew exactly what she was thinking. He threw her a brilliant smile, and then stood up and walked from the room.

McKenzie didn't allow herself to dwell any further on Byron Knight. She had a lot of work to do before Monday, and there was no time like the present. She would prove to herself and to Byron that she knew her stuff.

And, more importantly, she would survive the challenge Byron was throwing at her. Not only survive it, but excel at it.

CHAPTER FIVE

WHAT IN THE hell are you up to now?"

"Excuse me?"

Byron had known he'd get this reaction from Blake. That's what big brothers did. But he hadn't been expecting the guy to come barging into his office at the crack of dawn to yell at him. He'd been hoping Blake wouldn't notice for quite a while that McKenzie had been there working in their Seattle offices.

Because Byron had her working in the office adjoining his own, his brother had been bound to see her, but since Blake had gotten married, he'd been working more and more from home — when he wasn't at a construction site, at any rate, or at one of the other headquarters.

Blake was a strange one, and he still loved to get his hands dirty and work up a sweat. All of the brothers did, actually, but Blake seemed to like it more than either he or Tyler did.

"You have McKenzie working here. Don't play stupid with me, Byron."

"Stupid?"

"Yep. You got it in one. In our last conversation, you told me that you despised the woman, and that you thought she'd screwed up my life," Blake said, hands on his hips as he glared at Byron.

It was only Wednesday, and McKenzie had been working there for three days now. Byron's luck at not being found out by his brothers was bound to have ended sooner or later, but he'd have been far happier if it had been a lot later.

"She opened up an accounting company," Byron told him. "We were in need of a head accountant."

He'd said that calmly. If only it were really that simple. Since she'd stepped into his office on Monday and the two of them had discussed his expectations of her, all he could imagine was stripping her down and throwing her across his desk. It was nothing too personal, he assured himself. It was only because he wanted to take ownership of her, mess with her in the same way she'd messed with his older brother. She would learn that a person didn't get away with messing with any of the Knight brothers without suffering the consequences. Infatuation, or whatever the romance writers of the world wanted to call it, had nothing to do with it.

Then again, the woman was good at screwing with people's lives. Maybe she had somehow cast some sort of spell over him. She was a…witch. That would make a lot more sense than all of these fantasies springing up of their own accord in his brain and points south.

Were the fates with him or against him? It was hard to tell. Before Blake could say, "That's utter BS," McKenzie stepped through the doorway, looking down at the papers in her hands, not noticing that Byron was in a deadlock with his brother.

The outfit she was wearing was appropriate to the office — she always played it that way — but he seemed to be finding something wrong with everything she was doing. His eyes were drawn to the top two buttons of her modest blouse. They were undone, and though not even a hint of her cleavage was showing, Byron was captivated, tantalized. He was hot to undo the next couple of buttons to see what she was hiding.

Subtle pink lipstick filled out her lips, making them appear more than kissable, and his pulse sped up as she moved closer. And her scent… He couldn't figure out what it was doing to him, but his hormones were running amok.

She looked up, and then a genuine smile appeared on those lush lips. "Hi, Blake. I've been hoping to see you, but I've been so busy that I haven't had a chance yet to seek you out."

She walked up and gave Blake a *very* unprofessional hug, in Byron's humble opinion. It had Byron grinding his teeth. Yes, he knew she wasn't after his older brother, but it still got to him. Still, how did he know that for sure? His head was spinning because he really didn't know this woman at all when it came down to it.

"Did you figure out the problem?" Byron snapped, making both Blake and McKenzie turn his way.

McKenzie's eyes narrowed at his tone, and Blake looked as if he wanted to punch him.

"Unfortunately, I think the problem runs deeper than a numbers issue. You have someone at the Boise office who is…shall we say, skimming a bit off the top. I've been over this and over this, and there's no other explanation.

If I were you, I would have an internal audit done. It's going to take quite some time to figure out exactly who, but from what I've been seeing, I've narrowed it down to three possible people. If you know your employees well, then you might be able to narrow it down further." Her tone was professional in the extreme, and it was putting Byron on edge.

That made no sense. He wanted a professional, didn't he? So why was it that no matter what she did, he still found himself irritated? Why did he still find himself wanting to punish her? Hell, he didn't even know which direction was up anymore.

"I'll look this over as soon as Blake leaves," he said briskly, hoping his brother would take the hint and go away.

"Maybe I should help you with that," Blake said, his expression changing as he looked between Byron and McKenzie.

Byron fumed. He in no way wanted his brother getting any ideas in his head about him and McKenzie. Hell, there was no him and McKenzie.

"Also, I thought I would have a couple of our employees come over for interviews later today or tomorrow if you're up for it, Byron. I know you're wary about trusting anyone else, but you'll see that I have a more than competent staff."

Byron's temper escalated even further.

With Blake standing right there, though, he couldn't refuse McKenzie's request, which appeared to be what she already knew. She was smart. He would have to give her credit for that. A person didn't get to where she was in life at such a young age without having some decent brains. But still, it didn't take a lot of brains to run a whorehouse, did it? No, it just took a lot of conniving. He would do best to remember that.

"I'm very picky, as you know," Byron said. "But go ahead and bring them in." He thought that sounded gracious enough.

"Of course." Her tone hadn't changed, but the expression in her eyes told him that she wasn't fooled — he wasn't going to give any of the employees a chance. He wanted her, and only her, working here. And they both knew it.

"That will be all for now, McKenzie. I'll call you in when I'm finished speaking with my brother."

It was more than obvious that Byron's dismissal rankled her, but she gave a slight nod of her head, turned on her heels, and walked stiffly from the office.

During those few seconds, the tension could have been cut up and deep-fried, and Byron almost smiled at knowing he was getting under her skin. She got beneath his thick hide so easily that it was more than fitting that he got to her as well. Turnabout was fair play.

"Did you forget that we own this company together?" Blake asked, clearly irked at Byron's attempt to shut him out.

"Of course not, but I'm the one who's over the accounting department," Byron said, hoping that would be enough to get his brother to back the hell off.

"Since when did we ever say something like that?" Blake asked, though he didn't look angry — he seemed more curious. That was worse.

"I've just been under a lot of stress," Byron told him. "I spent too much time away from the offices and now it's catching up to me."

"Hmm."

"What the hell is that supposed to mean?" Byron fumed.

"You seem awfully upset," Blake said, and gave him an assessing look.

"I'm not some damn specimen for you to place underneath a microscope, Blake!"

"I'm not the one getting upset over nothing, Byron."

"Don't you have work to do?" Byron practically yelled.

Blake was quiet for several moments, and for the first time he could remember, Byron felt like squirming in his seat. What was wrong with him? But Blake's next words absolutely infuriated him.

"So, I'll ask you this question again; Why is McKenzie working here?"

"I already told you that we needed to have the position filled."

"She runs her accounting company. She doesn't fill in personally," Blake pointed out.

"Well, the job called for her and only her," Byron said. He was getting sick of defending himself.

"You're playing with fire, Byron. You *will* get burned," Blake said, a knowing smirk now on his face. "Badly burned."

"She's just filling in for a job, Blake. Why don't you stop trying to look any further than that and stop trying to play the shrink with me? We promised years ago that we wouldn't pull that crap with each other." Byron was fuming.

"Just don't play games with her, Byron. She might put on an act that she's strong and independent, and she certainly isn't weak, but she has some wounds, some deep wounds, and you do have the power to break her," Blake told him.

"Why don't you stop worrying about her? Just worry about your own life, you're your own woman," Byron snapped, very done with this ridiculous conversation. He didn't even realize that the way he'd worded that would suggest that McKenzie was *his* woman.

"I understand now. I can see that you're struggling with the way you're feeling, so I won't take offense over what you just said. But be warned, brother, that she's a friend of my wife's, and if you put her through hell, I'll be forced to step in and knock you down a peg or two."

"I would love to see you try, Blake. It's been a while since I've had a good brawl."

"All right, then. We'll talk about this later."

Before Byron could reply, Blake walked out into the hallway, and then Byron found himself grinding his teeth together when McKenzie's sweet laughter drifted in through his open office door. She never laughed around him, but maybe that was because he never tried to make her laugh. Making her happy wasn't on his agenda.

He waited a while to be sure his brother had returned to his own side of the building. Then he decided to make the woman — that *maddening* woman — wait even longer. He wasn't in the proper mood to work with her right now. So he tried to push McKenzie from his mind by digging into other projects on his computer.

It was much easier thought than done.

CHAPTER SIX

WHEN BLAKE LEFT her desk, McKenzie didn't know what to do. Byron had said he wanted to bring her in to discuss the Idaho files, but twenty minutes passed and he still wasn't calling her in. She felt flustered and out of sorts, but she wasn't the type to sit around and do nothing. She needed to pull herself together.

The last few days had been almost surreal. Yes, she knew that Byron's demanding she work at his company was his way of trying to control her, trying to punish her. He didn't actually believe his irrational allegations that she had ruined his brother's life…or did he? Business was business, and she'd come in Monday morning, gotten her assignment from him, and then he hadn't brought up anything personal — not once. He confused her, and she wasn't easily confused.

A few times when they were working together she would look up to catch his piercing gaze focused on her, but she almost thought she was imagining it, because the second he noticed her looking, his face grew unreadable. Not a trace showed of what he was feeling or thinking — if he felt or thought anything at all, that was.

That was fine with her. She didn't want to dance this particular dance from his perverse playbook. She just wanted to run her business, make a new start for herself, and let her past life go.

Byron wasn't making that easy — not one little bit.

There was a darkness about Byron that called to her on some basic level, whether she wanted to hear the call or not. Inside, she was just as messed up as he was, and there wasn't a chance that anything could ever work between the two of them. Even knowing this, though, she wondered what it would be like with him in the bedroom. Strange —sex was not something she would ever enjoy. But just being alone with the man sent jolts of electricity all through her body. And that kiss…

Oh, that kiss had melted her inside and out. McKenzie was sure he was a phenomenal lover — but all in self-interest. The woman never got the same pleasure from the dirty deed. But none of that mattered. Nothing mattered but survival. And no matter what people thought of her, she wasn't a whore. Yes, she'd run a business where she sold women to the highest bidder, but she'd done so to protect them. And that story was none of Byron's business.

And since Byron had not an ounce of empathy in his entire body, she was certain that he wouldn't care to hear her story anyway. He'd deemed her evil before he'd even met her, and he was inflicting his own method of punishment on her. But here was the thing —even though she was exhausted working what looked to be sixty-hour weeks for him, and then putting in as many hours as possible at her own business, he was actually helping her, because in the end, when she could show that Knight Construction was a client of hers, she would have people pouring in through her own business's doors.

When Byron still didn't call her into his office, she decided she'd best get at least some work done — something that wouldn't require her total concentration. Looking down at her paperwork, she sank into the numbers and forgot about her woes for at least a few minutes.

When her phone rang twenty minutes later, it gave McKenzie a start. Her plan of not sinking into work hadn't gone over so well, because she wasn't the type of person who could do half a job. She took pride in whatever she did, and she always gave it her all.

When a familiar number showed up on the screen, she smiled her first genuine smile of the day as she picked up. "Good morning, Zach."

"Morning, beautiful. How's it going in the real world?" he asked, his natural humor coming through, making her really miss her office.

"It is what it is," she replied, sending the file she was working on to the corner of the computer screen. "How are things going at our company?"

"It would be a lot better if you were here, and you know that, but I think I've got a handle on things. Did you talk the boss into letting anyone come in for interviews?"

Did Zach sound hopeful?

She shuddered. "Please tell me there isn't a disaster going on that you're too afraid to tell me about."

"If there were a disaster, McKenzie, I'd tell you, even if I didn't like it. I'd probably send flowers, actually, with a note that said our business is going down in flames, but since that isn't happening, you have nothing to worry about. Again, did the boss agree to interviews?"

"Yes, sort of," she said, though she had more than just a feeling it was a waste of time.

"Great. When can I send in Jim? I can do it now, if you like."

"Let me talk to Byron. But I don't think we should send in Jim. Let's bring in Mary. I think her personality would be a lot better fit here."

"Are you sure?"

Mary was sixty-eight, and she was a master accountant, flawless in her work. She was also a no-nonsense kind of woman. If Byron didn't like her, he wasn't going to like anyone.

"Yes, I'm sure. I think they would get along just fine," she said. "Hang on." Before he could reply she placed him on hold, took a deep breath and walked into the lion's den.

Knowing that Byron liked to exert his dominance, she waited until he looked up before she spoke. He was well aware she was in the room, but he could be a real jackass if she interrupted, and she wasn't going to chance it. He made her wait for a full sixty seconds before he finally looked away from his computer screen. Maybe she should have told Zach she'd call him back instead of making him listen to elevator music for minutes on end, a good chunk of his life that he would never get back. Oh, well. It was too late now. If he got busy he'd hang up and she would call back.

"I'm sorry to get in the way of your busy schedule, Byron, but I have Zach on the line, and Mary — I've told you about her — is available to come in this afternoon if you can make the time." McKenzie was brisk and impersonal, matching the way Byron spoke to her.

His eyes narrowed just the slightest bit, and then a small smile tilted his lips. "Bring her in now." He then looked back down at his computer.

He was dismissing her as if she were trash. Every time he did that, she felt her fingers clench into fists. She hated that he felt he needed to be so rude. She'd worked before in a business where she'd needed to keep her guard up at all times, but she'd never treated people as callously as Byron Knight treated her.

She hurried back to her phone and told Zach to send Mary over ASAP. She then paced the hall as she waited for her to show up, her nerves screaming until the woman walked around the corner.

If Byron liked Mary, this game could stop and she'd be free to go away and attend to her own business. McKenzie wasn't foolish enough to think he'd stop tormenting her that easily, but at least it could be done after business hours.

Though Mary had arrived quickly, Byron made her hang out in the sitting area for nearly an hour before bringing her into his office. McKenzie didn't even attempt to get anything important done while she waited for the woman to walk back out. If she had been a nail-biter, she would have been down to stubs. That she knew for sure.

Only fifteen minutes into the interview, when Byron's door opened and Mary stepped out looking less than pleased, McKenzie knew this wasn't going to work. She could send in a hundred people, but Byron wasn't going to hire any of them. He was only wasting all of their time right now.

Still, she had to ask. "What do you think, Mary?"

"I don't understand how you can work for that man. He sat there stone-cold and asked me a few questions, then stared at his computer screen for a while before thanking me and sending me on my way. I have never been so insulted, in my life." Mary had one hand on her hip, and she was clutching her briefcase with the other one.

"He might just be having a bad day. You're exceptional at what you do, Mary. Once he's had time to think about it, I'm sure he'll realize that you are exactly what's required for this job."

McKenzie was hoping and praying that she wouldn't lose such a valued employee over this. Mary could have retired five years ago, but she worked because she loved to do it. She was a widow and said it was much nicer to be out with other people than to sit at home alone hoping for a visit from the grandkids.

"I don't know that I would accept at this point," she said. "I enjoy coming in to work. And the past two months at *your* business have been satisfying. I have a feeling, however, that I wouldn't enjoy coming in here at all, even if it were only for a few weeks."

And with that, Mary turned and walked out.

Crap! Going to the bathroom first to refresh her lip gloss and take some deep breaths, McKenzie then made her way back to Byron's office, pausing outside his door before stepping inside.

This time she didn't wait for him to acknowledge her presence. "That was sure a quick interview," she said with too much false cheer in her voice.

"She wouldn't be a good fit."

Gritting her teeth, McKenzie counted to ten before

saying "Why?" The bastard kept using the phrase *a good fit*.

"I can read people, and though she has an excellent curriculum vitae, she wouldn't be a good fit for Knight Construction."

"Is anyone going to be a good fit?" she finally asked.

He gave her a hint of a smirk, and he looked into her eyes, freezing her where she stood across from him. "Not right now they won't, McKenzie. You're stuck here for a while."

A shudder passed through her. She was never going to survive this. With no way to respond to his statement, she finally wrenched her gaze away from his mesmerizing eyes and left his office.

The day wasn't even halfway over and she desperately needed a drink. Happy hour couldn't come soon enough.

CHAPTER SEVEN

HER EYES BARELY open, McKenzie pulled into her driveway and sat in her car for a few minutes. She needed to paste a smile on her face and pretend she wasn't burning the candle at both ends. Long ago someone had told her that if you smiled past the pain, you would eventually give a real smile, so it was her goal to turn her lips up no matter how upset she was. She also needed to remember that there was a reason she was doing all of this.

She was barely able to pull herself from the car, and she felt a rumble in her stomach as she dragged herself up the short path to her front door. She fumbled around on her keychain until she found the right key, then slipped it into the lock and turned it. But before she was able to open the door, a voice spoke that sent chills down her spine.

"You're looking mighty fine, McKenzie."

That voice! For years that voice had given her nightmares, had haunted her in ways that she feared would never go away. She had hoped she'd heard that voice for the last time, had changed cities, had done all she could to avoid it — the voice belonging to the man who had ripped away her innocence. Who had turned her into the woman she was today.

Anxiety instantly filled her, but she wouldn't give him the satisfaction of showing it. He was a part of her past that she had prayed that she'd never face again, but didn't she know the past was never forgotten?

Turning, she found him with a lit cigarette dangling from his puffy lips, and her eyes widened. Though the voice was exactly the same as she remembered, the man was almost unrecognizable.

Time had not been good to him.

In the last ten years he had grown larger, and it was in a bloated, beached-whale kind of way. His eyes had also changed. They were dull and lifeless — drugs and alcohol had obviously not been kind to him. Those eyes moved up and down her body, and though he was trying to appear relaxed as he leaned against the rail at the bottom of her porch, she could see the twitch in his fingers and other subtle hints that he was high on something but flirting with withdrawal.

"It's been a long time, Nathan," she said between clenched teeth. She was afraid that if she unclenched them, they would begin to chatter, and that would show the man weakness. Not acceptable. But what was he doing at her home, her refuge?

"It would have been much sooner, but I lost track of you after you ran away. I've searched a long time. You can imagine my surprise when I found out you were running a top-notch whorehouse," he said, a gleam lighting up his eyes, but just barely. "I was disappointed that the doors were closed by the time I was able to get here. I would have loved to have tasted your offerings."

She was sure he would have. But he couldn't have afforded them, even in his "prime." And never in a million years would she have inflicted that kind of man on her girls. "I'm surprised you didn't know I ran it. After all, you were the one to show me the ways of the real world, weren't you?" Her temper was escalating the more he looked at her, spoke to her.

"Now, now, McKenzie, I'm not feeling very welcomed right now. Why don't you invite me in for a nice drink so we can reminisce about old times?"

How had she ever found him attractive? How had she ever fallen for his lies?

"I told you the last night we were together — if *together* is the right word — that I never wanted to see you again," she reminded him. Yes, she was slightly afraid of him, and she had reason to be, but she wasn't about to stand there and pretend she felt anything for him but disgust. Dealing with him had always been a lose-lose proposition, and that hadn't changed.

"Ah, those are just words spoken in a lovers' spat, baby doll," he said, his lips twisting up in his sick attempt at a smile. The man never smiled, not really, not with any warmth. He had once been a predator of the most despicable kind, and she'd been unlucky enough to find out too late. But now she wasn't sure he was capable of taking care of himself, let alone of going after more innocent young women.

"Please tell me why you're here." McKenzie's exhaustion had returned, and it was overwhelming her. Not good. The last thing she wanted to happen was to pass out. She'd done that once in his presence, ten years ago, and the results had been unthinkably horrific.

"You stole from me, McKenzie. I want what's owed to me."

McKenzie's mouth dropped open at his words. She couldn't have possibly heard what she thought she'd just heard. Not a chance. She was silent for several moments as he squirmed on her bottom step and she gaped at him.

"Would you care to repeat that?" she said, her voice colder than ice.

He shifted again and broke eye contact, as if unable to face her wrath. He was pathetic, but she wasn't foolish enough to underestimate a desperate man. While speaking with him, she had pulled out her pepper spray, gripping the small bottle in her hand, ready to use it if necessary.

"You ran away with the money from that night…" He trailed off at the outrageous gasp coming from her, but he had to add, "My share as well as yours."

"I took nothing from you, Nathan," she said tightly. "And if I were you, I wouldn't dare bring up that night." Cold fury — or was it hot? — was pouring through her.

Desperation must have begun to make him brave, because he straightened up at her words, and his eyes darted around, maybe searching for witnesses. She didn't know. But if he took one step toward her, she did know that he would regret it.

"That's where you're wrong, sex kitten. I spent time and money on you, trained you, prepared you, and then got you a good first job. And the thanks I got from you was that you ran away in the middle of the night with my money. That, in my book, is theft."

"I didn't know I was being trained," she reminded him.

"I never asked for that."

"Ah, but you see, don't you, that you used what I taught you to create a very successful business."

"I no longer run Relinquish Control," she said.

"It doesn't matter. From what I found out, you ran it for several years, and your…clients paid a lot of money for the whores you trained. I would think you'd want to give me a little bit of your take as a thank-you."

"Are you kidding me?" she gasped. He might as well sprout two heads right now, because she considered nothing as unbelievable as what he'd just said.

He shrank back the tiniest bit at her show of outrage, but then he stood back up and glared at her. She had to be careful. A desperate man equaled a crazy one. Her fingers gripped the pepper spray a little tighter, her finger on the trigger.

"There's no way you'll ever get a single dime from me. Do you understand?" Rage was the only thing keeping her on her two feet right then.

"You do owe me, McKenzie, and you *will* pay it — one way or another."

His eyes drifted up and down her body, making her stomach turn. Never, ever would this man touch her again, not while she was still breathing.

Nathan now made a big mistake — he took a step toward her. McKenzie didn't budge an inch. She stretched out her arm and blasted him with the pepper spray. The man who had been responsible for the most nightmarish night of her life let forth an ear-piercing scream, and he stumbled back down her front steps and collapsed on the ground, grinding his hands into his eyes.

"You bitch!" he screamed over and over again as he

writhed in agony. McKenzie wasn't going to take another second of this. Reaching for her phone, she dialed the police and sat at the top of the steps, her eyes not moving from his twisting body.

After about fifteen minutes, he lay there in the fetal position, crying. She still didn't trust the idea of taking her eyes off him. When the police showed up ten minutes later, she took her first deep breath.

The next forty-five minutes were some of the longest minutes of her life. She watched Nathan being cuffed and placed in the back of the squad car, and then she answered the officers' questions before they finally drove away.

She didn't know whether she'd seen the last of that… slimeball, but she would be a fool to underestimate him. He looked to be out of choices, and that made him dangerous. She wouldn't stroll down any dark alleys anytime soon.

Once inside her house, she engaged the locks, and then she moved determinedly through the place, checking every window. When she had assured herself that everything was locked up tight, or seemed to be, she went to her bedroom and collapsed across the bed.

The tears finally fell, and she curled up into a ball on top of her blankets and cried out her frustration. She should have known it would never be over with a man like that. How had she ever been such a fool as to trust him?

Now there were two men in her life who wanted the impossible from her.

CHAPTER EIGHT

A BEAD OF sweat dripped down Byron's neck as he took a break and leaned against the wall of the building he'd been pounding with a hammer. No, he didn't have time to be out on the job site. And no, he wasn't running away from the office, where he'd brought in a woman who was making his life a living hell.

Okay, maybe he was running from that woman. He was a fool – a certifiable fool. He could admit this in his own head. He'd had her working for him for a week. At any time, he could hire one of her employees and see her maybe once or twice a year if she happened to be at his brother's house when he was. End of problem. But the thought of doing just that turned his gut inside out.

Absurd, simply absurd.

"We're heading to lunch, boss. Do you want to join us?"

Byron turned to see his foreman waiting by the work truck and the rest of the men piling into varying vehicles as they got ready to go in search of food. "No. I'm going to finish up what I've been working on and head back to the offices. I've already wasted too much of my day," Byron told him.

"It's never a waste to work up a sweat," Wyatt said before jumping in the truck and taking off.

Byron moved to his own truck and pulled out a bottle of water from the cooler, then sat down under a tree not too far from the building. The place was going up fast and it was a beauty. A new mall was being built on the outskirts of Seattle, far enough away to not feel like the city, but close enough to get to, and the owners wanted it to have a historic feel to it with several architectural features that he didn't often get to do anymore. All three of them had been working on and off on this site, since it was such a pleasure to work on.

Closing his eyes, he leaned back feeling a small measure of peace. He did love his business, loved working with his brothers, and loved being independent from someone being able to boss him around. If he could only quit obsessing about a certain woman, his life would be damn near perfect.

Opening his eyes after a few minutes, Byron noticed horses out in the field. What the hell? Where had they come from? They were looking at the opening to the building, and Byron turned, then froze at what he saw.

"McKenzie?" he called, but she only smiled and gave the smallest shake of her head before holding up a finger against her lips.

Byron stood, to move over toward her, but again she shook her head, and then those delicate fingers of hers lifted, resting on the top button of her blouse, and Byron's body instantly froze.

Looking him in the eyes, she moved her other hand

up, and then her head tilted back and her fingers traveled down the front of her blouse as she moaned aloud. Byron was instantly rock solid. He took a step toward her, but her head came back up and she shook it a third time.

Fine. If she wanted to play, he would let her play. He stepped back and leaned against the tree, his body pulsing, his eyes glued to McKenzie as those fingers rose again and she slowly began undoing her blouse, one small button at a time. Finally, he would see what her clothes kept hidden from him. As her full breasts were revealed to him, it was everything he had imagined and more, with her dark pink nipples jutting out.

She didn't wear a bra to work? Now that was going to make him even harder when he was at the Knight Construction offices. His eyes shifted to her waist as she reached behind her and undid the zipper at her back and then the skirt was dropping to the ground.

No panties, either? Whoa! Byron feasted his eyes on her uncovered womanhood as she kicked the skirt away, then spread her legs and leaned against the doorway of the building, her chest pushed out, her ass dipping low as she opened and closed her legs.

Enough was enough.

Slowly, he moved forward. Her head turned as she looked at him, a come-hither expression playing in her eyes. "Is this what you've been wanting, Byron?" she asked as she stood back up and faced him, one hand high on the door, as she leaned there and waited for him to reach her.

"Oh, this and so much more," he whispered huskily. "You're making me burn alive."

"It is a very warm day," she said, lifting her free hand to her neck and letting it travel down between her breasts and then along the plane of her stomach. She stopped at the top of her incredibly sexy mound.

"It's certainly getting hotter," he gasped as her finger dipped lower and circled the very part of her body he wanted his mouth to devour.

"I'm getting lonely here, Byron," she purred as she reached out toward him.

She didn't need to say anything more. Byron closed the small gap between them and pulled her roughly against him with his arms. His head descended and he finally tasted her sweet lips. He plundered her mouth, his hands reaching down and gripping her backside, pulling her against the roughness of his jeans and the straining hardness of his arousal.

She reached around him and grasped his hair with both of her hands as she groaned into his mouth, begging him for more. He would give her anything she wanted — anything at all.

Her kiss was filled with promises of what was to come, and he accepted what she was offering, making his own silent promises of what he would do to her, with her, for her. This woman was making him come unglued, and he never wanted to put the pieces back together again.

She pushed her hips against him, her leg lifting behind him, her foot caressing his calves as she tried to get closer. "Clothes. They need to come off," she panted before connecting her mouth back to his in a passionate display of possession.

With an urgency born of pure desire, Byron's knee went between her thighs, and he pushed her legs apart. Then he dropped to his knees, his head resting for a moment on the silk of her stomach as he inhaled her sweet scent. "So perfect, so beautiful," he said with reverence.

Grasping one leg of hers, he raised it onto his shoulder, spreading her wide open for his view. Without any further hesitation, he leaned forward, finally getting his first taste of her heat, and he nearly released inside his pants.

His tongue swiped up and down the soft folds of her womanhood, and he sucked the pulsing flower of her core, her cries of pleasure telling him how fast or slow to go. He worshipped her body, learned every inch of her most tantalizing area, before he could take no more.

Releasing her, he stood, and in less than a minute, his clothes were tossed aside. "I need to take you now, McKenzie," he told her.

"Finally," she gasped, her eyes looking down, pleasure filling them at the sight of his throbbing erection. "It's all mine," she said then looked back up and licked her lips.

Their bodies met together without him feeling any movement, and then he was lifting her, and soon her tight heat was surrounding him, her perfect core holding him inside her.

"Oh, Byron, more," she cried out as she laid her head on his shoulder, her teeth sinking into his skin. He didn't care. The pain grounded him just enough not to explode inside her.

Still, he moved faster, gripping her derrière in his hands as he cried out her name, seeking release for both of them. Leaning down, he licked the salty skin of her neck and sucked on the point where her pulse was thundering.

"Please, Byron…please…," she moaned. "I need…"

The feel of her breasts sliding against his chest, her legs gripped tightly around his hips, her mouth caressing his shoulder. It was all too much. "Let go, McKenzie, let go," he cried out, his own pleasure building.

"Yes, now!" she cried as her body held him tight…

"Wake up!"

Byron shot upright, confused, hard, and not knowing what in the hell was going on. He looked around, his eyes trying to adjust to the bright light. Where was McKenzie?

"What in the hell were you dreaming about?" one person asked.

"I don't know," said another, "but I'll have what he was having." Laughter accompanied that comment.

With a groan of frustration, Byron realized he'd fallen asleep beneath the tree. To make matter worse, he must have been saying something unfortunate, because his crew was back and they were enjoying his pain.

"You might want to go and find the girl and get some satisfaction," his foreman said with a big guffaw.

"Go back to work, Wyatt. I'm heading to the offices," he grumbled.

As he walked stiffly back to his truck, trying desperately not to show the men how painful this walk of shame was, he thought finding the girl was a damn good idea. It was time that they closed on *this* deal.

CHAPTER NINE

MCKENZIE WAS LATE getting back to work. She wasn't in the best of moods to begin with since her miserable "boyfriend" of long ago thought it would be fun to torment her. No, she wasn't afraid of him, but he probably figured if he pestered her enough, she would give him what he wanted to make him go away. He was almost right about that.

She couldn't see how even as a young and vulnerable nineteen-year-old she could have been attracted to that man. What in the world was wrong with her? As soon as she had that thought, sadness enveloped her. Of course, there was something wrong. How could she ever forget?

No. This wasn't the time or the place to think of the past. But the past was continually in her face. Though deep regret filled her with that thought too, she had to remind herself that at least she was living her life. Even if she had encountered some bumpy roads along the way, she'd been able to handle those roads without utter disaster.

It wasn't that way for everyone.

Again, she had to shake off the depressing thoughts, and then walk quickly back to the offices. When Byron had come in yesterday, he had been in a foul mood, snapping at her and everyone else. Today, luckily, he'd been in business meetings with his brothers all morning, so she hadn't had to deal with his foul mood so far. She was going to be more than happy when she was free of him. She had enough to worry about without dealing with a man prone to such incredible mood swings.

Slipping back inside the Knight Construction office building at about quarter past one, she made her way to her desk, where she clicked on her computer and tried to return to work mode. When she heard a shuffling noise and looked up, she found Byron's standard scowl, and it was harder to deal with than normal.

"I thought you were going to take this job seriously," he said.

"Of course I am," she replied.

"Then why do you find it acceptable to take over an hour for lunch?"

What the heck? Was he timing her? A freaking billionaire? She hadn't been on the clock in a lot of years and no one had ever questioned her work ethic. She'd always worked over the clock. But she wasn't going to argue with him.

"Is there something you want, Byron?" she asked with a sigh.

"Yes, for you to do your job and do it right."

That was just plain rude!

"I *am* doing my job. Is there anything else you want?" She was losing what little cool she had left, and she still had most of the afternoon to get through. Most of the afternoon *and* two and a half more weeks.

He paused for a moment before speaking again. "Get the Boise papers gathered. I want to go over that situation in an hour." With that he turned and walked away.

McKenzie had to take a deep breath and then another before she pulled up the files. She would go over them one final time, of course, so she would have every detail on the tip of her tongue. Yes, right there on her tongue… The last thing she wanted was to have him think she couldn't do her job. All she needed right now was to get fired and to have her company's reputation ruined before it ever had a chance to really take off.

Then again, maybe that was exactly what she needed. She could start fresh in a new place. But how was that going to help her? She'd discovered years ago that she couldn't run from her problems — no matter how much she wanted to. She could escape for a while, but inevitably, even if it took years, her problems would once again find her.

Before she could dive into work, her phone rang, and instead of ignoring it, she glanced down then cringed when she saw the number. This wasn't the time to deal with more problems, but she knew there was a good chance he'd come barging through the doors if she ignored him. They had only kept him in jail for three days after he'd trespassed, telling her sorry, but he hadn't committed a crime. He'd called her every day since. He wasn't too good at taking a hint, so after much hesitation she picked up the phone.

"I'm not going away, McKenzie. As a matter of fact, I'm hanging out at the park right across the street from where you work. You know you can never be too careful when you're out walking. Things can happen to a person."

"You don't scare me, Nathan. You're pathetic and weak, and no matter how much you bug me, I'm not caving into you, so please just go back to the hole you crawled out of and leave me the hell alone."

"I *should* scare you," he said, but he couldn't quite pull it off.

"I don't have money to give you, but even if I did, I would rather burn it in a dumpster on the side of the street than give you anything I earn. Are you hearing me?"

"You may have got the drop on me once, but it won't happen again."

"Maybe if there weren't such a little-boy whine in your voice, your threats would come off as a lot more effective," she said. The thing was, that even though he was a pathetic excuse of a human being, she couldn't forget he was also desperate.

"I have nowhere else to go," he said.

"It's not my problem—"

He hung up on her, and McKenzie let out a sigh while rubbing her forehead. How many more problems could she take before she exploded? She was soon to find out, because it looked like they were going to just continue to pile up on her.

McKenzie sat there and concentrated on her breathing for several moments before she realized she wasn't alone. She didn't want to look up, didn't want to know how much of the conversation Byron had heard. She was going to lose this job for sure, and then she would have even less than she had now.

How much had he heard? His expression gave nothing away. She was silent as she waited to hear what insult he was going to skewer her with next. Hell, he might as well bring it on. Her day couldn't get any worse.

"My office...now," he told her, and he turned and walked out.

He didn't need to say anything further. She knew only too well what men expected when they used that tone.

She rose from her chair slowly and took a step in the direction of his office before her shoulders went back and a bit of the fire that had seen her through many hard times flared up inside her. She was sick of getting bossed around, sick of men trying to control her. Wasn't that the reason she'd opened the doors to Relinquish Control in the first place? To bring control back into her life.

Instead of following Byron blindly into his office, she grabbed her purse and made her way to the women's restroom around the corner from her office. And she took her time. She washed her face, the cool water feeling incredible against her heated skin, and reapplied her modest amount of makeup. Then she propped herself up against the sink and stared at her image.

"You are McKenzie Beaumont. You have survived so much, and you will continue to survive. No one can make you feel inferior. No one but you can decide your course of action. No one can trample on the life you have made for yourself. Bullies are bullies because they can't earn respect any other way. Deep down, they're cowards."

This was a speech she had delivered to herself many times in the course of her life, and she had a feeling she'd say it many times more. Yes, she wasn't immune to fear, and yes, she'd have weak moments — everyone did — but no, she wouldn't let those moments define who she was. And she wouldn't allow anyone to keep her down for long.

With her head held high, she left the restroom and headed back toward Byron's office. Her armor was back in place and she was going to keep this job. She was going to make a success of her new business and beat back Nathan Guilder, damn him to hell. He was nothing more than a weak man trying to make up for his tiny dick.

McKenzie nearly smiled at her thoughts. That was until she stepped into Byron's office and saw the way he was looking at her. This wasn't going to be her easiest battle.

Not her easiest battle by a long shot.

CHAPTER TEN

J UST WHEN BYRON thought he had a clue about who McKenzie Beaumont was, something happened to throw his suspicions into disarray. He didn't know her at all.

She was a mystery, and hadn't he decided already that he was going to figure her out, find out what made her tick, and make her pay for meddling in lives she had no business meddling in? Yes, that was exactly what he'd decided, but he couldn't fathom why all of the sudden he gave a damn about her.

That phone call she'd been on had changed not only her voice but her entire demeanor. Byron knew when someone was scared — and though McKenzie was obviously irritated, she was also afraid. He *would* find out why. He might have believed it was an act except that she hadn't known he was there. She wasn't acting for his benefit.

So what was going on in her life?

"Who were you talking to, McKenzie?" Byron had

learned long ago to not let his opponents have time to think. If he caught her by surprise, she wouldn't have time to make up a good lie. He was pretty miffed she'd managed to get away for the twenty minutes between the phone call and coming to his office. It was enough time to build a likely-sounding story, so he needed to be quick on his feet now.

"It was no one you'd know."

"Hmm. Try me. I know a lot of people."

"Trust me, Byron; you don't know this person," she said.

"Whoever it was seems to be wanting something you're not willing to give," he said, and by the widening of her eyes, he could see she'd hoped he hadn't heard the entire conversation — her half, anyway. But it was too bad for her.

Byron didn't want his opinion of McKenzie to change. He wanted to think of her as cold, calculated, and interested only in herself, but he couldn't help but notice the frightened look in her eyes, or the way she was so carefully holding herself together. But he found himself wanting to be her Knight in shining armor, or an Armani suit, ready to rescue her from whatever dragon had been on the other end of her phone line.

"I'm here to do a job, Byron, and it's a job that could be handled by any number of people I know. But I'm still here, and I'm doing this job well. If I take a call, that call is none of your business," she said, her eyes connecting with his and showing him that she certainly had some steel in her character.

Byron's pulse started to speed up. He shouldn't feel anything like rage now. Nothing this woman did should upset him, but he was so frustrated with himself and with her that he found himself wanting to grab her, shake her, and get past that icy composure she inevitably reverted to.

Instead of doing any of that, he fired off more words in a voice that was, if possible, icier. "You should be grateful you are working here, and for what I can do for your new company's reputation."

"I *am* grateful, but my *personal* business is still none of *your* business."

"When your personal life spills over into the working environment, it becomes my business," he told her. "Definitely my business."

Her eyes narrowed as they remained in a silent deadlock, both of them refusing to back down. Then he saw the telltale slumping of her shoulders, and he knew he'd gained a minor advantage over her.

"You are right, of course. I'll make sure to keep my phone put away while working."

Though she'd said the words, she clearly didn't mean them. There was something going on in her life that she had zero control over, and if it was the last thing he did, he'd find out what it was. But short of shaking the information from her, he didn't know how in the hell he was going to get her to speak.

He should just leave it alone and let her deal with her own messes. Whatever had happened, she surely had brought it on herself.

But words slipped from his mouth. "I can help you with whatever is going on." Sheesh! That hadn't been what he'd meant to say at all.

"There is nothing going on. I don't need your help."

McKenzie had spoken between clenched teeth, and

he watched as her fingers closed into fists as she tried desperately to regain her cool and her composure.

Byron never — absolutely never — offered to help anyone, particularly a woman, and to have that offer thrown back at him so haughtily infuriated him. But they said nothing else for several moments; they were spending the time staring daggers at one another.

"Dammit, McKenzie! This is ridiculous," he huffed, ticked that she was making him back down.

"I won't say it again, so listen up this time. I don't need any help from you, Mr. Knight."

And for just a moment, he thought he saw a slight sheen spread over her eyes, but it was gone so quickly that he was sure that he must have imagined it.

Distance wasn't doing the trick, so with his will to stay away from her gone, he began moving across the room, drawing closer to her. He had to give her points for not retreating. He saw the new look in her eyes, saw that she wanted to turn and run, but her stubborn pride wouldn't allow her to do that.

"I heard your end of the conversation, McKenzie. You *do* need my help." He stopped right in front of her, forcing her head to tilt up so she could continue looking at him.

It might have been the wrong move for him, because now her subtle scent was drifting over him, her warm breath brushing his throat, her body heat practically burning him. This woman was certainly casting a spell over him, and he had a feeling the spell wouldn't be broken until he captured her lips, captured her body, and purged her from his system. Especially after his incredibly vivid dream the day before — he'd woken up from it hungry and wanting and in the worst of moods.

"Even if I did need help, I wouldn't ask for it," she said. Her tone held only a trace of vulnerability, but just that small measure of helplessness made him want more than ever to pull her into his embrace.

When her helplessness evaporated and in its place a taunting smile filled her lips, the small strand of elastic that was holding up his will to resist her snapped. Snaking his arms around her back, he drew her to him and at long last kissed her again.

When she melted against him, he pulled back. "You can't stop me from doing what I want," he said. What did that mean? Was he speaking about helping her or bedding her? Maybe both.

And his lips claimed hers again, preventing her from hitting him with a comeback. He'd expected her to fight him, expected her to protest, but she didn't lie to either of them, didn't put up a front. Instead, her hands came up to rest on his arms as she opened her sweet mouth to him and he thrust his tongue inside, claiming her in a way he'd been dreaming of doing since that first kiss five months earlier. And even more so now, since his dream.

A sigh escaped her mouth, but he caught it. His blood raged as his fingers dipped over the curve of her derrière and he tugged her hips against his pulsing erection. He wanted there to be no doubts at all in her mind about what she was doing to him. He hadn't had sex in a long, long time, and it was showing.

Yes, they would be incredible together. Still, as much as he needed a woman, this woman wasn't the one he should feel any desire for. He should just be playing a game with her, not giving her power over him.

Anger at her — at him…hell, he didn't know — gave

him the strength to break contact. He took a step back, then another, just to force himself not to drag her into his arms again.

Power.

This woman had it in spades. He didn't know whether she truly comprehended her power or not. She was beautiful, sensual, and the most fascinating woman he'd ever met, and yet there was something behind her eyes, something that scared him. But it beckoned to him, too.

"Some things just shouldn't happen," he drawled.

"I fully agree," she said, her lips slightly trembling.

Finally, a smile spread over his lips. He was rethinking everything. "The kiss wasn't what I meant shouldn't have happened, McKenzie," he whispered as he moved across the room and leaned against his desk. He was enjoying her obvious confusion.

Yes, the only way to exorcise this female demon was to deal with the sexual tension. They were consenting adults, and they both wanted this. So why not see it through? He'd been tempted long enough with those thoughts.

"I don't understand you," she said, and she took the smallest step backward, a sign of fear and weakness. She seemed to notice the gesture, and she stopped, her shoulders firming once again, her eyes narrowing.

"There's something going on here, and it's not going away. The logical conclusion is to relieve the ache." His tone and his eyes revealed nothing — he was very careful about that.

"Is this what you mean, Byron? Should we just climb on your desk and screw like bunnies?"

"A little crude, McKenzie, but that could be arranged. Still, I'd prefer to be outside the family headquarters when

I…never mind." If he hadn't been rock hard before, he was now as he pictured doing what he'd stopped short of telling her.

"So what if we consider each other desirable? So what if you turn me on…on occasion? I still think you're an asshole. Just because my body might say I want you doesn't mean the rest of me will go along."

He wasn't fooled. "I *will* enjoy taming you, McKenzie," he said.

She was silent for a moment before she raised her hand to her hip and looked around the room. "How long do you need, Byron? Five minutes? Ten? Surely not more than that. With you acting like a hormonal teenager, I'm sure if I just bend over your desk, you could be done before the second hand reaches one minute."

Her spate of words only intrigued him more. She was obviously used to getting her way, used to dominating men and making them pant at her feet. That went along with her territory. She played football, so to speak, so she must use offense as a quick defense to get out of tight situations. *Tight.*

She'd never dealt with him before.

"That's a start," he told her. "But I'd need a lot more time, Trust me on that. Have you ever heard the phrase 'the best sex you ever had'? I'll be that and more. I guarantee it."

She took a deep breath, and then her eyes glazed over, shutting him out. He knew they were done with this for now.

"I will gather all the reports you needed," she said, and she turned to walk away.

Before he realized what he was doing, he stepped away from behind his desk and caught her in the doorway. He rested his hand on her shoulder and skimmed his lips lightly across her neck.

"This will happen," he murmured.

A shudder passed through her, and she walked out of his office.

Byron sat back down, his pants way too tight, his erection throbbing. And yet he still felt satisfied somehow. He couldn't wait for the next round of this epic fight between the two of them.

It was a few minutes later when he realized she'd managed to distract him from finding out what her phone call had been about. Dammit! But he'd let her try to keep her little secret from him for now. In the end he would learn exactly what was going on, and whether she wanted him to or not, he would help.

Only because he needed her to do her job, he assured himself — not because he actually gave a flying…fig about the woman. That lie hung in his brain while he got back to work, but he allowed it to remain there, because that's how he excused himself for his erratic behavior.

CHAPTER ELEVEN

AFTER FINISHING UP the last of her work for the day, McKenzie tried to hurry. It was nearing six-thirty and she had a dinner date with Jewell that she didn't want to miss. It was the best part of her week lately. She stood up, collected her coat and purse, then wavered on whether she should tell Byron she was leaving. She was well past quitting time, so she didn't need to ask permission, but as only the two of them were left on this floor, it would be polite to let him know she was heading out.

The choice was taken from her when he stepped through the open doorway, his coat hanging from his fingers. They hadn't spoken since the kiss — the second one — not even to go over the Boise papers. She found herself…nervous. It was a strange sensation.

"It's late and I'm starved," he said, blocking her only exit. "Why don't we get something to eat and finish the discussion we began earlier?"

There was no way she was going to get back into that

discussion. They would fight, he would kiss her, she would fall into his bed. She wasn't a stupid woman, and she pretty much knew the way this was all going to end if she weren't very, very careful with what she did and said around this man over the next few weeks.

"We finished that discussion," she told him as sweetly as possible.

"No, not to my satisfaction," he countered, and he didn't budge an inch from the doorway.

"Sorry, boss." She had to remind him of his position and hers before continuing. "I have dinner plans. Maybe some other time." She scooted a few steps toward the door, hoping he would move out of the way.

He didn't.

"What are your plans?" His voice didn't change, but something in his eyes did, and if she were a stupid woman, she might have thought he was jealous. But that was just absurd. He might want to bed her, but he had no feelings for her — no good ones, anyway — and certainly didn't feel anything strong enough to cause him jealousy.

Still, she didn't want to push him — not with the way he'd been acting around her. And not with the weakness she seemed to suffer from when in his presence. She'd surely lose any major fight they got into.

"I'm going out with Jewell," she told him, and the sharp look in his eyes faded. Hmm. Interesting.

"Where's Blake?" he asked, though she was sure he knew. Then again, maybe he didn't.

"This is a ritual for us. At least twice a month we meet up, unless a natural disaster occurs. So Blake uses it as an excuse to have a boys' night, or do whatever it is that men do when their wives aren't home," she said.

"A boys' night?" he said before his lips turned up. "Please tell me what a boys' night consists of."

"I don't know. I just…I just said something. I have no idea what he does when we have our dinners. I just know that he doesn't complain about it, because he's not over-the-top possessive." She *really* wanted to get around him and go to dinner.

"Invite me to join you."

"What?" Had she heard him correctly?

"It's rude to make someone repeat themselves, McKenzie."

"You're calling *me* rude?" she gasped. "You just tried to invite yourself along to a girls' night. You are probably the most insanely rude person I've ever met?"

"I didn't call you rude; I said it *was* rude to make someone say something more than once, which you're making me do again."

"Ugh." She threw up her hands in frustration. "I'm leaving now." She finally braved walking up to him and brushing past. He stepped back and their gazes collided as she moved around him.

A shiver racked her body as she turned away and began walking toward the elevators. His devilish eyes, rock-solid body, and kiss-me lips had her stomach churning, and it would be disastrous for her to remain in his presence for too long. So why was she suddenly feeling guilty that she hadn't caved in and invited him to dinner? It was ridiculous.

She had absolutely nothing to feel guilty about. He'd gone beyond rude when he asked her to bring him to dinner with her girlfriend. But she couldn't shake from her mind the millisecond when it had looked like disappointment was clouding his eyes.

He wasn't really disappointed. He just wanted to interrogate her — that was all. If Byron wanted a dinner companion, he could open up his little black book and find a thousand people to go out with him. Heck, a thousand was a gross understatement. A man like him had to have a million dates on call.

So when she found herself turning around and moving back toward his office, she wanted to slap herself. What in the world was wrong with her? She'd made a clean escape. All she'd had to do was to hit the down button on the elevator and then be free of Byron for the rest of the night.

Instead, she found herself in his doorway, and she was for once the one to look in on *him* without *his* knowledge. He was leaning back in his chair, and for one brief moment he looked so vulnerable to her, so different from the hard man he always presented himself as, that she couldn't stop herself from saying words she didn't want to say.

"Would you like to come to dinner, Byron?"

He seemed startled as he turned her way, and just like that, any traces of vulnerability disappeared. "I thought you'd never ask," he said, standing and picking up his coat.

Grrr. Yes, she was a fool. Why in the world had she locked herself into a social setting with this man? Obviously she'd just done exactly what he wanted her to do. When they stepped into the elevator, a space that was always sufficiently roomy when she was traveling up and down it with anyone other than Byron Knight, she felt claustrophobic.

After only a couple of weeks of working by this man's side, he was messing with her head in a way that she'd never allowed a man to mess with her — not even Nathan, who was the scum of the earth. She could blame what had happened with Nathan on her youth and inexperience. What in the world could she blame her erratic feelings for Byron on? Nothing came to mind.

Just when she thought the silence couldn't get any louder, Byron spoke, waking her up out of her reverie, and she focused on the steel doors in front of her. "I'm going to the Boise offices next week. I need you to be there."

Every instinct in her body told her she had to get out of this. "I already gave you all the information you would need for this trip. My presence isn't necessary." There. That had come out without emotion. She was good.

"You can't read faces through a picture, McKenzie. You're the one who has narrowed this down to a few individuals. Now, we need to finish it and get the Boise offices running the way they should be."

That had almost sounded professional, all business and nothing more. She might have bought into that if it weren't for the earth-shattering kiss the two of them had shared — and, of course, his confidence that she would end up in his bed.

"Honestly, Byron, I don't think I'd do anything other than slow you down. I'm great with numbers, but not so great with people," she said, though it was a lie. She could read people well, which is why Relinquish Control had been successful.

"I think you're being too modest. I won't force you to go, but I will let you know that if we can solve this matter quickly, it would look much better for our company…and, of course, the reputation of yours."

Ohhh, that was a low blow. Her job performance had been flawless up till this point. She wanted to question him, find out what he meant by that statement, but she also already knew. Or did she? The Knight brothers were always honest, even this one.

So, when she found herself nodding at him, agreeing to go with him, she began to wonder about her own motives. Did she want to be alone with him? "Okay, I will accompany you. It's only a day trip, correct?"

The elevator doors opened and he placed his hand against the door while she walked out. Then he followed her. "If all goes well, McKenzie, we can be in and out of the offices in a few hours," he said.

That hadn't been what she'd asked him, but when he put his hand on her shoulder as they exited the building, McKenzie forgot all about what she'd been planning to ask him next.

Never before had a man had the ability to silence her when she wanted to speak — not without drugging her first — but, with Byron, she seemed to be in a constant daze. This so wasn't where she wanted to be. Not where she wanted to be at all.

If she didn't pull herself together, and soon, she'd be in deep trouble while working and playing games with Mr. Byron Knight.

CHAPTER TWELVE

T HE AIR WAS cold, as usual, as McKenzie and Byron made their way down the busy Seattle sidewalks. "Was it your idea to walk?" Byron grumbled as they turned a corner.

"You aren't going to melt from a little bit of moisture. It's ridiculous to take a cab or drive a few measly city blocks," she said, huddled up beneath her coat.

She'd been so flustered leaving the offices, she'd forgotten to grab her gloves, so she stuffed her hands into her pockets There was no way she was going to admit to Byron that she was in the least bit cold, though. Not after calling him a wuss. She would, however, pick up the pace a little bit.

When she stopped in front of a dingy-looking place, she caught Byron's eyes before she stepped up to the door.

"Here? Seriously?" he asked.

"Look, buster, you're the one who weaseled a dinner invite out of me. Now, if you want to join us, you're stuck eating where we like," she said, reaching out to open the door.

Byron jumped forward right before her fingers connected with the handle, and he opened it for her. Noise from inside blared out, and McKenzie had to smile. Although it wasn't exactly posh, she had eaten at the place many, many times, and the food was one of the best-kept secrets of Seattle. The head chef was a personal friend of hers now, as she probably ate there more often than the owners did.

"I'm fine with this place," Byron said as she went past him, mumbling a thank-you because he'd opened the door.

"You don't appear to be fine with it," she pointed out, her stomach dipping the slightest bit when her body brushed his. He had purposely left her hardly any room to get by him.

"I was just thinking we'd be going somewhere a little more quiet."

"Ha! You mean you were hoping to go to a place a lot more fancy."

"You're putting words into my mouth," he said before leaning down, leaving her zero personal space as his eyes bored into hers. "If I want something in my mouth, you'll be the first person I tell."

She was frozen as his breath washed over her face. The noise, the crowded front area, the people — *everything* disappeared except for him and those irresistible lips.

McKenzie was grateful when a group of college kids came up behind them, bumping into Byron and pulling McKenzie from the spell she'd been under. She'd been just about ready to let him kiss her right there in a crowded room full of strangers and servers who knew who she was. She really needed to pull herself together or she wasn't going to last even a few more days, let alone two more weeks in this man's presence.

"This way," she told Byron, and she began moving through the crowd. Jewell would already be there, guarding their favorite table, and with luck she'd have a drink ready and waiting. McKenzie really needed that drink if she planned on getting through this dinner in one piece.

The back corner of the place offered almost a measure of privacy — almost, not quite — and there, Jewell sat, a virgin daiquiri in front of her and a cold mimosa on the opposite side of the table. Thank goodness!

"Sorry I'm late, Jewell," McKenzie said.

Her friend gave her an easy smile before her eyes widened as she took in Byron.

"Um, no problem…," Jewell replied, leaving the words trailing off.

"Good to see you, Jewell," Byron said easily. "McKenzie took pity on me since we were working late tonight and I haven't had a thing to eat all day."

Byron leaned against McKenzie so he could reach around and pull out a chair. As her blood raced, she lost her thoughts again, and almost plopped down into the chair instead of sitting down properly.

When Byron sat next to her, she had to bite her lip. Had she been thinking, she would have slid in next to Jewell on the side of the table with a bench, giving herself some much needed space away from Byron. But then, of course, she would have been forced to look at the man during the whole meal. She wasn't sure which setup would be worse.

She looked at Jewell and could see a myriad of questions in her friend's eyes, but Jewell compressed her lips and then gave Byron a gigantic smile.

"It's good to see you, Byron. You work so much, and your brother complains that you don't come over more often."

"I'll have to change that," he said.

Just then, the waitress, Marsha, appeared, notepad in hand and eyes glued to Byron. "I haven't seen you in here before," she said, her cheeks flushed slightly.

McKenzie made eye contact with Jewell and rolled her eyes just a bit. What was it about good-looking — okay, incredible-looking — men that turned normal women into drooling messes?

"Well, if the food turns out as good as it smells, I'll have to become a regular…Marsha," Byron said, after looking at her name tag. He practically beamed at the waitress, irritating McKenzie even more than she'd already been at the whole ridiculous situation.

Marsha giggled, actually giggled, making McKenzie roll her eyes again. But as Byron turned to give the waitress his full attention, his leg brushed against McKenzie's, and her agitation turned into raging hormones. She tried to pull away from him, but he just pushed a little closer, and she couldn't find an escape.

"What can I get you to drink?" the waitress finally asked, as if knowing she'd been staring for too long.

"I'll take a Jack Daniel's, straight up," Byron replied, and the waitress practically fluttered her eyes before rushing away to fill his order.

"It must be nice to fluster people like that," Jewell said with a laugh, and Byron turned to her with his eyebrows raised. "Oh, come on, Byron, you had to have noticed the way our waitress was drooling all over you. And she's normally sane."

"I have no idea what you're talking about," he said, but McKenzie knew he was very aware of his effect on people — on women in particular.

"I'm starving," Jewell told them, "so please figure out what you want to eat. We should get our orders in before the rest of the people now piling through the doors."

They were silent for a few moments as McKenzie stared at her menu, not seeing a thing on it. Thankfully, she was a creature of habit and already knew what she wanted for dinner, so she wouldn't be required to use her brain for a few moments.

When Byron set his menu down, he captured Jewell's attention. She threw him back an amused look that McKenzie had no doubt was meant to irritate her. It worked.

"So, Jewell," he asked point-blank, "are you going to tell me what's going on with McKenzie? What is she so desperate to hide from me?"

McKenzie gasped in outrage. "There's nothing going on," she told him before Jewell could say a word. She then looked sternly at Jewell before turning back to Byron. "And if there were something going on, Jewell would remain loyal to me and not spill my secrets."

From the mischievous look on Jewell's face, McKenzie had a sinking feeling that her friend wasn't above selling her out. She'd been with Jewell when one of Nathan's calls had come in, and though she'd tried to cover it up as much as possible, she was shaken up, and Jewell voiced her concern. At least he hadn't shown up at her door.

"I know you women like to stick together and all, but if McKenzie is in trouble, don't you think it would be in her best interests to have as many people helping her as possible?" Byron asked, reaching across the table and patting Jewell's hand.

McKenzie wanted to punch him. "I will repeat that *nothing* is going on," she practically growled.

"I think your friend likes to keep secrets," Byron remarked to Jewell. Then he turned and looked at McKenzie, first making her want to squirm in her seat, then ticking her off. He was making her feel like a scolded child.

"She isn't sharing with me either right now, Byron. If she were, and if I felt that she needed help, I would have to agree with you," Jewell told him, surprising McKenzie.

"Okay, I can accept that," Byron said, before he got a mysterious look in his eyes and turned back to Jewell, a megawatt smile suddenly on his lips. "Is she dating anyone?"

Both women went silent for a moment when that question came out. McKenzie was the first to recover. "Don't you dare answer that, Jewell," she ordered, but it was Byron she glared at. "I am working for you right now, Byron, for some strange reason, and I care about doing a good job. But my personal life is *none* of your damn business."

He shifted again, his leg completely glued to hers, and though she wanted anger to remain her main emotion, it wasn't. He leaned down close, way too close, his expression unchanging, and he spoke only when he knew she was completely tuned in to him.

"I want to get to know you more, learn every…little… thing about you. This thing between us *is* personal. If you can't take the heat, I suggest you walk away right now," he warned her.

It took a moment for McKenzie to say a word, and then her shoulders came back and she glared back at him. "And if I do?"

He was silent for so long that she didn't know if he was going to answer, but then his lips, which had tightened with his last words, turned up again, this time in a far more conquering smile, which scared her. Be my guest, McKenzie. I'm not forcing you to work for me."

She hesitated a moment and then glared at him again. "Yes, you are. You completely bullied me into the job."

"I'm a businessman, McKenzie, and I know how to get what I want."

"And if I walk away now?"

"You have free will," he told her. "Do you want to walk away?"

McKenzie forgot that Jewell was sitting there across from them as she looked into Byron's eyes. Did she want to leave? That was the million-dollar question. She should want to leave, want to get as far away from him as she possibly could. But is that what she really wanted?

She couldn't say the words that might set her free. And she didn't understand why not.

"I didn't think so. You're just as curious as I am about what in the hell is going on between us," he said before turning his attention back to Jewell. "So, tell me, when was McKenzie's last relationship?"

He went on as if they hadn't just had a spat, a tense moment, or whatever in the hell they'd had. McKenzie was so much in shock at his interrogation of her friend, she didn't protest this time.

That mischievous light returned to Jewell's eyes.

"I honestly don't know," she said. "I haven't ever seen McKenzie with a man."

Byron's hand came up and rested on McKenzie's leg, and though she wanted to remove it, she also loved the way it felt there.

McKenzie had good reason to hate all men — she actually prided herself on feeling that way. And even though she knew Byron's intentions were far less than honorable, she couldn't shake the pull she felt toward him.

She was in more trouble than she could handle. And it seemed that it only got worse each new day. Her thoughts were interrupted when the waitress came and took their food order, then disappeared again after flirting, of course, as much as possible.

Luckily, Marsha soon returned to bring refills on their drinks, and the tension was broken. The conversation turned to more neutral topics.

Byron was giving McKenzie a reprieve.

But McKenzie knew the reprieve wouldn't last.

CHAPTER THIRTEEN

BYRON COULD SEE the tension rolling off McKenzie in waves. This was exactly where he wanted her, wasn't it? So why did he find himself backing away? He should be going in for the kill, but instead he found himself sitting back, eating away at his pasta Bordelaise and sipping on a good red while McKenzie talked to Jewell and slowly calmed down.

Jewell wasn't paying attention to him, so he took the opportunity to look at her, really look at her. She didn't seem like the money-grubbing whore he'd thought she was. Whenever Blake's name came up, no matter how subtly, she practically glowed. He didn't like having his beliefs tested. But he knew this: even if Jewell was indeed the hooker with a heart of gold that Blake believed her, a young woman who went into the escort business to help her young brother, that didn't make McKenzie any less contemptible. She was the real whore of the two. She ran the upscale escort service — so upscale that Blake had paid a quarter of a million bucks to bed Jewell the second time around, and McKenzie pulled in half. That woman was the embodiment of money-grubbing.

But if Jewell was an exception among women — if she really did love his brother, and they were good for each other — was his vendetta against McKenzie valid anymore? What was her former profession to him? What was *she* to him? Just another bad woman in a long line of them.

He wasn't sure what his motives were any longer. All he knew was that he wasn't ready to let McKenzie walk away from him yet.

The only certain thing about his life was that he didn't do relationships. Yes, he liked sex, and yes he liked companionship, but he didn't do the whole boyfriend-girlfriend thing. He didn't hold hands and stroke the woman's ego. Look at what that had gained his father — death. A weak man in the clutches of a female who was no better than a prostitute.

But these thoughts weren't quite helping. Even though he'd only been with McKenzie a short time, she was getting under his skin. Why? She wasn't playing games with him, or he didn't think she was playing games, but still, something was going on. That was it. There was a mystery here, and that was what was driving him. He would get to the bottom of it because he couldn't stand to be left in the dark. And that's exactly where Byron felt he was at the moment.

"How is everything?" Marsha asked, all her attention on Byron.

"The pasta bordello…" He paused and looked pointedly at Jewell to which she sent him a withering glare and he simply winked. Then he gave his full attention back to

Marsha. "Sorry, my mistake. The pasta Bordelaise is some of the best I've had."

"That's wonderful to hear. I'll let the chef know," she said with a giggle before finally retreating.

They finished their meal and when the check came, Byron snatched it up and paid it all, including a generous tip. When the two women protested, he just smiled as he stood and held out a hand to McKenzie. Would she refuse his help up?

She accepted his hand with obvious reluctance, and he tugged, pulling her off balance just enough that she stumbled into him. His damn hormones got into the act again, and he looked down into her eyes, needing more than anything else right then to kiss her. Byron didn't normally do public displays of affection, but everyone seemed to fade away when he was touching McKenzie. Dammit!

"Do I need to call the fire department before this place goes up in flames?" Jewell asked.

"What?" McKenzie asked, flinching.

Jewell giggled. "The way the two of you were looking at each other, I think you were both going to spontaneously combust at any minute."

Byron was grateful for the interruption. He normally didn't let anyone know what he was feeling, even when in lust. Besides, when he next kissed McKenzie, he intended to finish what he started, and he certainly couldn't do that here, in a crowded bistro.

"I have to get going, McKenzie, but I'll see you next week. We *will* talk before then," Jewell told her with a meaningful look. She said goodbye to Byron and went ahead of the two them out of the place.

It wasn't long before Byron had McKenzie to himself again as they walked down the street back to the offices where their cars were parked. "I enjoyed Jewell's company this evening," he said, surprised that it was true.

"She's very difficult to be around without enjoying her company," McKenzie replied.

"The two of you started out as employee and boss. How did you become best friends?" he asked, and she stiffened with that reminder of how she and Jewell had met.

She was quiet a moment before answering. "I honestly don't know. It didn't take me very long to figure out that Relinquish Control wasn't the right place for her, but by then she'd already spent a week with your brother and then had come back even emptier than the first time I'd met her. Over the next few months, we talked, a lot, and friendship just grew."

"I think I could actually like Jewell if I spent much time with her."

"Yes, you could like a lot of people if you gave them a chance." Her voice was suddenly so sad, and he needed to know why.

"What is happening in your life, McKenzie? Why all the mystery, and all the secrets?"

"I have nothing to hide," she said, shutting him down immediately.

"Not true, McKenzie. I watch you," he said, and her eyes widened. "And I listen. You're in trouble, and you think you can handle it, but I've seen you be strong and I've seen you frightened. Sometimes it really helps to get it out." Why in the hell was he suddenly acting like Dr. Phil?

She stopped and faced him. "I'm very capable of taking care of myself, and I'm not so foolish as to think that you and I are friends, or ever could be friends. I know what this is, Byron. I'm a puzzle, and you can't stand not being able to solve me. The bottom line is that I'm not worth solving. You would find all of this very anticlimactic in the end," she said with a fake laugh. *Damn. She shouldn't have suggested the word "climax."*

She resumed walking, and it took Byron a moment to move his feet and catch back up to her. "I understand that you're capable of taking care of yourself, but I *am* involved now, and if you think I'm one of these new age weak men — a quiche eater — you are sadly mistaken. Haven't I said this before? When I want something, I always get it." He took her arm and kept her from entering the building when they reached it.

"Sometimes in life, I'm afraid to say, you just have to accept that the world isn't always in the palm of your hand," she told him. "You don't get to know my secrets, and you don't get to control me. I'm not yours to manipulate."

Byron was done with words. Frustration brewed inside him, and he knew of only one way to release the tension. Before she had time to blink, he pulled her into his arms with the intention of plundering her mouth. That would keep her from arguing.

One hand slid behind her neck and the other around her back as he tugged her close to him, demanding immediate surrender.

She didn't disappoint him.

As he slipped his fingers beneath her jacket and began moving them up her side, he had one thing in mind, and only one thing, and that was to feel her breasts and find out whether they were as soft and pliable as he'd dreamed about.

A car driving past backfired before he could find out, and she sprang from his arms, her breathing heavy, her eyes bright with desire. Dammit! He'd forgotten where they were once again.

"Let's finish this in private," he said.

She took another step back before speaking. "That's not going to happen," she whispered, and Byron could barely hear her above the city noises.

"We both need this, McKenzie. Quit fighting it." He wasn't normally a man to beg, but right now he was almost willing to drop to his knees if that's what it took to get her to come home with him.

"It doesn't matter, Byron. I'm used to denying myself what I need," she said, a sad smile on her lips.

"You can only deny yourself for so long before you simply fade away," he told her.

"I think I'll take the risk," she said. He moved toward her, but she backed up, turned away toward the parking garage next to the building, and made her escape.

Yes, he could have chased her down and probably kissed her into submission long enough to get them both satisfaction, possibly even on the hood of her car, but for some reason he didn't go after her. She'd said no. As much as he didn't want to, he needed to respect that.

He went into his building with heavy feet. If he wasn't going to get laid, he would work until his eyes hurt, and if that didn't do the trick, he'd leave and beat himself up in his home gym.

Yes, he wanted to bed McKenzie, but what surprised him was that he didn't want to destroy the woman anymore. Why not? It couldn't possibly be because he was growing attached to her. Byron refused to attach himself to anyone.

Especially a woman who had a secret or possibly many secrets. A woman who'd run a bordello. That was nothing but trouble.

CHAPTER FOURTEEN

BYRON TOOK A deep breath as he pulled up to the office building where Bill Berkshire had a modest setup. The man had formally retired years ago, but he'd needed something to do in order to keep from going insane after the death of his wife.

The old codger was a royal pain in all the Knight brothers' asses because he wouldn't let them take care of him. He insisted on living in a run-down house, for example, and they had to fight him every step of the way to keep it maintained.

Bill had been a friend of Byron's grandfather, who'd also been a wonderful man, and when Byron's parents died, Bill and Vivian had been the ones to step up and take care of them. Byron knew for a fact that the old man had at least a few million dollars sitting in his bank account from that time so long ago — money he'd been assigned for acting as the boys' guardian — but the man had refused to touch the money, saying it was tainted. He hadn't wanted anything that had come from the boys' parents, not after what those two had put the rest of them through.

As much as Byron loved Bill, he wasn't looking forward to this particular visit. Bill hadn't told Byron why he was summoning him, but Byron wasn't a fool. His damn brother must have called Bill and told him that Byron was harassing a young woman. That's the only interpretation Byron could put on the stern tone Bill had used when he'd demanded he come and talk with him immediately.

Of course, Byron could have said he was a busy man and couldn't come by right then, but he'd never do that — not in a million years. Bill was one of the few souls on this earth for whom Byron — hell, all the brothers — would drop everything, no questions asked.

Even if that meant suffering through a long lecture.

Once inside the ten-story building, Byron began moving toward the elevator. He'd been to Bill's office many times before. But several businesses leased space in the building, and before he got too far, a woman stopped him.

"May I help you?" she asked, and Byron wondered if she was supposed to be security. He kept his amusement to himself. A woman security guard wasn't someone he would fear. Maybe some would say he was a sexist pig. He couldn't care less.

"I'm just here to see a friend," he said as he attempted to walk around her.

"You must not have been here in the last sixty days…," she began, but when his intense gaze zeroed in on her, she choked on her words.

"What does when I have or when I haven't been here have to do with anything?" he asked, trying to hide his irritation. By the rounding of her eyes, it didn't appear that he was doing a very good job of that.

"Um…it's just that…we…um…have new security protocols now. Everyone has to check in at the…um…what's that called?" Her cheeks flushed.

"Front desk?" he asked with as little sarcasm as he could manage.

"Yes, I'm sorry. I'm not usually so…I don't know…at a loss for words," she gulped, her shoulders going back as she tried to regain her composure.

"Fine. I'll check in," he said. He wasn't happy to be doing so, but, then again, it was the same at his own building.

"It's just that we had a robbery a little while back and the people in the offices wanted better security," she rushed to explain as she walked next to him to the front desk. And there was his reasoning of why a woman couldn't be a security guard. She could barely speak, let alone take him down if he decided to get violent.

"I understand." He was fed up with all these explanations.

"Thank you," she breathed as they reached the desk together.

"Byron Knight here to see Bill Berkshire," he said with crisp efficiency.

"One moment, sir," said the man behind the desk, and he lifted his phone.

"You're Byron Knight — *the* Byron Knight of Knight Construction?" the woman gasped, giving him no choice but to turn his attention back to her.

"Yes. Do I know you?" he asked, giving her a second glance. He didn't recognize her, but that didn't necessarily mean anything. He would bet there were a dozen women he could pass on the street who he'd taken to his bed who he wouldn't recognize a month later. They meant that little to him.

"No…not really, but my brother has worked for you for three years and talks nonstop about you and your brothers and about what a great job it is. I applied at your building a couple of times, but I haven't been called back," she said, looking up at him hopefully.

"I don't do the hiring," Byron told her; that was his typical statement when people approached him about work.

"Oh, I wasn't implying anything," she hastened to say, but he could see disappointment filling her eyes as she smiled up at him weakly.

To his amazement, Byron felt a twinge of guilt, as if he should at least offer the woman an interview. What in the world was wrong with him?

"You're all cleared to head up to the eighth floor, Mr. Knight," the desk attendant told him. "Here's your visitor's badge."

"Thank you." He turned and moved away from the desk and the woman.

"It was very nice to meet you, Mr. Knight," the woman said, her eyes flaring the tiniest bit as she reached out a hand and touched his arm lightly. This was a change in the way she was playing things. She was now letting him know she was available if he wanted to ask her out on a date.

He said nothing else as he moved to the elevator. It was best to let her know he was neither interested nor available. Maybe a few weeks ago, and a few months ago for sure, he would have flirted a bit, seen if she piqued his interest at all. But since he'd kissed McKenzie Beaumont not only once but on four separate occasions now, other women held no appeal at all for him.

He wanted only one woman in his bed. And within the next few days, that's exactly where he was going to have her. He hoped like hell his hormones would then simmer down to more manageable levels and he would stop acting like a damn teenager. Why did the term *blue balls* keep occurring to him?

It was a short elevator ride to the eighth floor, and then Byron went around the corner to Bill's office. He would honestly love to know what Bill did all day — maybe the old man just played solitaire on his computer. Whatever made him happy was all that mattered, and if sitting in a downtown office was what he wanted to do, then Byron would continue letting Bill think the rent hadn't gone up in four years and that he was paying fair market value on the space. He would never know that the brothers had made a deal with the manager of the building and that they were the ones ensuring that the old fellow stayed where he wanted to be.

When Bill looked up, Byron could have no doubt he was on the man's naughty list — the old man was positively glowering at him. Okay, he probably deserved it for the many things he *did* do wrong on a daily basis. So he would take the verbal abuse and hopefully act humble enough to leave on Bill's good side.

He decided to wait and see what Bill would say before he spoke. He didn't have to wait long.

"What in the hell are you doing playing games with a fine woman like McKenzie Beaumont?" Bill asked gruffly, glaring at Byron from behind his desk.

"It's good to see you as well, Bill," Byron said as he moved forward and took a seat in the chair facing Bill.

"Don't you patronize me, boy. I helped to raise you, in case you don't remember," Bill grumbled, and the words Byron had heard for his entire adult life made him smile.

He'd never said he loved anyone out loud — that brand of silence ran in the Knight family — but without a doubt, he had love for this man — this gruff, grumpy man who was probably the only reason Byron had any humanity left in him at all.

"I'd never think of doing such a thing, Bill," he said. He was trying not to smile too wide, or Bill would think he was laughing at him, and that was not the case at all.

Bill looked at him suspiciously for several moments before he spoke again. "I asked you a question, Byron. Don't think you can smile up at me and make me forget why I called you here."

"What have you heard?" Byron certainly wasn't going to spill his guts if the man didn't know anything more than a rumor or two.

"Your brother told me how you went after this nice young woman who is the reason he met Jewell, and that he's worried you're going to hurt her. I've met McKenzie, and I agree with Blake. She's a beautiful young woman and she doesn't deserve to be harassed by the likes of you," Bill said, his glare not flickering.

"I'm not harassing her," Byron said. There was no one else he would actually defend himself to. Usually, if someone spoke to him this way — and it didn't happen often — he would simply get up and walk away. He would never treat Bill with disrespect like that, though. He'd take whatever the man had to dish out.

Besides, he was in a little shock at wondering how in the world McKenzie had managed to bedazzle someone as savvy as Bill. The woman had run a flipping bordello for damns sake. She certainly wasn't a saint, and he wouldn't describe her as a nice young lady. She must be even craftier than he had given her credit for.

"You certainly won't be anymore," Bill said, enunciating each word.

Byron was silent for several heartbeats, and then he sighed. He didn't want to give anything of himself away — he never did — but he suddenly felt as if he had zero choice. If he didn't give Bill something to chew on, this could get really ugly.

"Look, Bill, it might have started out with me… harassing her, but it's different now. I…I can't get this woman off my mind. I can't sleep, eat right, or even think on most days. I just…I don't know." Byron rubbed his hand across his hair. Even knowing everything he knew, he was infatuated to a certain extent.

"But you're making her unhappy, so maybe you should back off. Maybe she just doesn't want to be with you," Bill said, but his voice was quieter as he observed Byron. That was the last thing Byron wanted, and his defenses popped right up, but with a lot of willpower he pushed them down again.

"She does," Byron told him. "Believe me, if I felt she had no interest, I would back off, but there's something between us, something that can't be denied. She's scared — and I don't know what she's scared of, but she's running, and it's not from me."

"How are you so sure it isn't you she's trying to run from? You Knight youngsters have always had big egos."

"I know when a woman has the hots…ummm…is interested in me," Byron said. He could be confident about that, above anything else.

"Is sex worth torturing this woman over?" Bill asked.

"It's not just sex…" Byron stopped himself before he said too much. This was going into a territory he refused to go into. "Sex is always worth anything," he said instead, but it was too late. The only thing that would make this any better for him was if he told Bill he just wanted to screw her brains out until she was washed from him mind and he certainly couldn't say that.

The words were too vile to let escape from his mouth, so instead he chose to be silent as Bill sat there and analyzed him. Byron felt as if he were under a microscope and he didn't like the feeling one little bit.

"Look, Byron, you got the worst possible example of what love should be like by watching your very messed-up parents. In the end your father was weak, and your mother — well, your mother wasn't…I shouldn't speak ill of the dead, but your mother was a cold-stone bitch," he said, sending Byron into shock. "It's just that you don't want to repeat those patterns. If you open up your heart, allow other people in, you can have a good life. Mistreating women isn't the way to do that."

Byron let out a bitter laugh as he looked at the only father…grandfather…uncle -—whatever he wanted to call him, he was the only male figure he'd had worth modeling himself after. "I'm screwed then, because I have no desire to ever feel love. Not after what I witnessed."

"I've had my own demons a time or two in my life. But while married to my beautiful Vivian, those demons were kept at bay. Every single day since I lost her, I've been fighting depression or whatever the shrinks call it. You need to open yourself up before it's too late, or you'll find yourself alone and filled with emptiness."

Bill's statement stopped the next words Byron had been about to say. Suddenly, the man who had always been there for him seemed so lonely, so much smaller, so frail. Was that really how Byron wanted to end up — alone, sitting behind a desk with nothing to do?

"Bill…" He didn't know what to say now.

Bill's shoulders went back as if just realizing what he'd said. "Don't you even think about offering me comfort, boy. I'm just trying to prove a point."

"And what point is that?" Byron asked.

"Don't be a fool," he said gruffly.

"I won't be," Byron said, and he actually meant it.

"Good. Then our meeting is over. Get out of here and don't keep screwing up. I won't be so easy on you the next time."

Bill obviously needed to protect himself now. Byron understood that, and it was okay with him. But he found himself doing something he hadn't done since he was a small child. When Bill stood up to walk him to the door, Byron went up to him and gave the man a hug, gently slapping his back before he pulled away.

Bill said nothing as Byron released him, and they made it to the door, but when Byron said goodbye and glanced at the old man's eyes, he could have sworn there was a slight shine there.

Was Byron really such a bastard that just the smallest act of kindness from him inspired tears? If that was the case, didn't he need to make serious changes in his life?

Maybe. And maybe he would do just that.

CHAPTER FIFTEEN

MCKENZIE GAZED HELPLESSLY at her computer monitor — it was one of the first times she could remember being unable to make sense of what she was seeing. It might as well have been a jumble of numbers dancing on the screen.

This was so not her day at work.

She hadn't suddenly lost her ability to read or suffered a stroke. There was only one possible explanation for her sudden ditziness: Byron Knight. He was a menace to society and he should be stopped.

One minute he was demanding and in her face, and then the next he was gracious and kind. She couldn't keep up with him, and it was throwing her for a loop. It was Tuesday, five days since the kiss on the street. He'd been gone on Friday, and then had come into the offices on Monday as if nothing at all had happened.

She felt as if she were going to start screaming at any minute, and she didn't like being this crazy, irrational person. She didn't like at all that she felt as if her feet weren't firmly planted on the ground anymore. She felt as if she were going to be carried away off into the atmosphere at any minute if her brain didn't get some density to it.

On top of that, she hadn't heard another word from Nathan, and though that should bring her joy, it worried her more than anything. Had he given up? She would be thrilled if that were the case, but she highly doubted it. She was just waiting for the ax to fall.

It seemed to be the story of her life these days.

In a perfect world, Nathan would disappear again and Byron would let her bring another of her accountants into his offices while giving her unlimited business and recommending her business to all of his friends.

But McKenzie had learned long ago that she in no way lived in a perfect world. With a sigh, she closed the program she was working on — or rather *not* working on — and leaned back in her chair. She wasn't going to get anything done, not anytime soon.

On top of every other emotion she was feeling, the kisses from Byron had awakened something inside her that she hadn't known she possessed— desire. She was feeling it more and more each day, and every time he walked by her, his subtle cologne drifting out to entice her, she felt that much weaker.

Looking at her watch, she let out a relieved breath to see it had finally hit five o'clock. With Byron not there at the moment she could actually leave at quitting time. Hallelujah. As she began gathering her things, Blake popped into her office, a friendly smile on his face.

"I was hoping I would catch you, McKenzie. If I'd messed up, Jewell would have had my head, but I've been on a conference call for the last hour," he said in greeting.

Seeing Blake cheered her instantly. "I'm on my way out the door, but if Jewell needs me to do something for her, I can try to fit it in, though I will definitely rag her for not calling me personally," she told him, cringing imperceptibly while thinking about all the work she needed to do tonight for her own business.

"Good," he said. "I need you to come over for dinner."

"I can't tonight, Blake. I have a mountain load of work to do." How she missed the days of having a work schedule that didn't remind her of a sweatshop, or a chain gang.

"That's why Jewell had me stop in instead of calling you. She is assured that my charm will win you over. Besides, everyone needs to eat." Blake held open her door as she approached.

"I know, but I really shouldn't." Still, she hesitated. It would be so nice to visit with Jewell for a while, maybe even get some time to complain to her friend, though she probably wouldn't do it.

"I refuse to take no for an answer. Jewell specifically told me to stuff you into my car to guarantee you didn't try to get out of it. She's worried about you," Blake said as the two of them began heading toward the elevator.

"Well, I guess if I'm being kidnapped…" Jewell stepped onto the elevator and waited while Blake pushed the down button.

"It's settled then."

The two of them chatted on the way down and she followed him to his car, promising herself that she wouldn't stay too late. She didn't want to spend the whole time at her friends' place feeling guilty about the pile of work waiting for her at home. At least she wouldn't have to clean up a mess after fixing dinner.

Who was she kidding? She would have been lucky to throw a frozen dinner in a microwave. Lately, her dinner of choice — actually, her dinner of necessity — had been frosted flakes or ice cream. She made up for that by having a protein drink in the mornings and a healthy lunch at work. If time permitted, she even made it down to the office gym and used the elliptical for twenty minutes.

Fifteen minutes later, they arrived and Blake and Jewell's house, and Blake called out to his wife. She called back and Blake led her down the hallway into the family room.

When they both entered, McKenzie froze. Sitting on the couch, looking more than comfortable was Byron, with Jewell's puppy biting at his toes, Justin sitting next to him, seeming to be in uncle idol heaven, and a big smile on Byron's face. The sight almost made her take a step backward. It was time for a quick retreat. No wonder he hadn't been at the office.

She thought for a moment about turning around and running back out of the house, but there was no way she could give away how much this man affected her. Jewell probably just hadn't thought about the awkwardness when she invited both McKenzie and Byron to dinner. After all, McKenzie had brought Byron to their dinner last week.

If only she'd taken the time to talk to Jewell after then, to let her know that Byron was the last man on earth she wanted to spend any more of her precious social time with. Too late now, though. She wasn't about to make a scene in her best friend's home.

"Evening, darling," Blake said as he walked right up to his wife and pulled her into his arms, kissing her like he hadn't seen her in months instead of hours.

"I missed you," Jewell told him before giggling as Blake pulled back.

His hand went to her belly. "Our son or daughter has a good, solid kick," he said, and he looked adoringly into her eyes.

"Just like their mother," she said with a wink.

"I'm famished," he said with a wicked smile that made McKenzie squirm where she stood.

What in the world was wrong with her? She had hosted an escort service! A few words shouldn't make her blush. Thankfully Justin saved them all.

"You two are disgusting, and you're forgetting there are other people in the room," he said.

Blake laughed before moving over and pulling Justin to his feet, giving him a hug, and then turning back to his wife. "Well, I'm hungry for real food, too," he said with a wink.

"You are terrible," Jewell pretended to huff. "But I guess I should feed you."

"You said your back was hurting not five minutes ago," Byron interrupted, and Blake instantly looked concerned. "Let me and McKenzie get the food together while you rest for half an hour."

McKenzie was so shocked by his offer to help, she didn't even take offense that he'd also volunteered her. If flies had been hanging around in the room, they would have buzzed right into her open mouth.

"You're guests," Jewell protested. "I couldn't have you do that."

"Of course you can. We're family now, aren't we?" Byron pointed out.

"Let me give you a back rub and see if that helps," Blake suggested as he began pulling her toward the stairs.

"I have a bit of homework to do anyway and I'd rather get it done before dinner so I can play on the X-Box after," Justin piped in, rushing from the room.

Jewell looked at McKenzie. "If you're sure you don't mind…"

McKenzie certainly couldn't beg her pregnant friend not to go and lie down, but, oh, how she wanted to. She wanted anything but to be left alone with Byron, especially doing something as domestic as cooking together. She should have tried much harder to refuse Blake's invitation to dinner.

"Go get some rest. We'll make sure you have a wonderful dinner" is what McKenzie ended up saying, of course.

Then Blake led Jewell away, and McKenzie found herself standing there awkwardly with Byron, the first time she'd been alone with him since after dinner in the bistro last week. The fates weren't in her favor right now. Even at the office, other people had been around.

"After you, McKenzie," Byron said, holding out a hand. She was left with no choice but to go along with him to the gourmet kitchen. "How was work today? I was solving a crisis on a job site," he told her as he looked in the fridge before he started to bring things out.

"It went smoothly," she lied, and she waited for him to tell her what to do.

When all the dinner fixings were on the counter, he looked back at her. "I'll do the meat if you want to get the salad ready," he said, and he began unwrapping the steaks.

"That's fine." She found a cutting board and began

dicing vegetables and putting them into a bowl.

Soon the two of them were moving around the kitchen together, and though it was large, McKenzie noticed that Byron was taking every opportunity possible to touch her. It was just a slight brush here, and their arms bumping there, but it was enough to drive her batty.

By the time he was letting the meat rest and whipping up a quick sauce for it, and she had the table set and the side dishes ready on the table, her nerves were stretched thin. She was more than ready for her friend to come back into the room and break up the tension. If Jewell didn't show soon, McKenzie was calling a cab and getting the heck out of Dodge.

"It smells delicious down here," Jewell said.

McKenzie whirled around when Blake and Jewell came strolling back into the room, Jewell's cheeks practically glowing. McKenzie's eyes narrowed in suspicion. Had her friend's back truly been hurting, or had it all been a pretense to leave her alone with Byron? Just wait till she got Jewell alone for five minutes!

"Thank you, Jewell. We've been slaving away," Byron said. He placed the meat on the table and then the four of them sat down.

"Yeah, I'm sure you had a rough time," Blake said.

"Don't you need to call Justin?" McKenzie asked as they all started dishing up.

"He's on an iPad chat with a school mate trying to figure out their group project so we told him to finish up and then he could grab frozen burritos. The kid doesn't like steak for some reason," Blake said.

"He likes what he likes," Jewell defended.

"He's incredible," Blake said, leaning over and kissing

her.

"How has this year gone?" McKenzie asked Blake.

Last year Blake had found out he was the father of Justin, who was Jewell's brother. It was long and complicated, but it had all worked out beautifully and McKenzie was really glad the three of them had found each other.

"It's been strange becoming a dad to an adolescent boy, but I adore him, and he's so damn smart. He'll be working in the offices in no time at all," Blake said, a proud smile on his face.

"As long as you don't make him grow up too fast," Jewell insisted.

"I've already missed too much. I wouldn't think of making him grow too fast," Blake said.

"This steak is fantastic," Jewell said when there was a pause for a moment.

"I have secret methods of cooking ribeye," Byron bragged.

"Yeah, you throw it in a pan and watch it sizzle," Blake said.

"Hey. I know how to impress in the kitchen," Byron insisted.

"That's not a room I've heard you brag about before," Blake countered.

The two brothers laughed, and Jewell looked at McKenzie and rolled her eyes. "Men. They are just not trainable," she said with a shrug.

"Or they're just crude," McKenzie added. Blake wasn't even shamed in the slightest about his past sexual exploits. That should be more than enough warning for her to stay away from him. But it seemed that if there was a chance of danger, she was the first one rushing forward.

"That too," Jewell said.

"Thank you both for doing this," Blake piped up. "Jewell felt much better after lying down for just a few minutes. Sometimes, it just helps her to get the weight off her back for a while."

"Of course. It was no problem," McKenzie told them. No problem if you like torture...

"How far along are you, Jewell?" McKenzie was surprised by this question. How could she know this and Blake not know?

"Six months already. I can't believe this child will be here in three months. I'm nowhere near ready," she said as she leaned back with a slight cringe. McKenzie felt bad because it was obvious that her back really was bothering her.

"I can't believe you have a son, and are going to be a dad again," Byron said. McKenzie couldn't figure out how he felt about that from his tone.

"It was something I vowed to never want. What a fool I was to ever think being alone was better than having a loving family," Blake said, looking pointedly at his brother.

Byron shifted in his seat, refusing to meet McKenzie's eyes. She really wanted to run more than ever before. This conversation was going in a direction she wanted to be as far away from as humanly possible.

Thankfully the topic changed from family and then the conversation flowed smoothly as the four adults had a nice meal. The brothers kept ribbing each other, and McKenzie was surprised when she found herself laughing at several things Byron said.

She was seeing a side of him she'd never gotten to see before — not that she'd had all that much contact with him, even in the past week or so, but still, she was shocked when two hours passed and it felt like fifteen minutes.

Justin flitted in for a few minutes, threw burritos in the microwave, then rushed back out again, saying they were still working on their homework. What in the world kind of homework would a nine year old have that required hours? Dang, school was getting harder.

"We don't let him do this every night. Normally we eat as a family," Jewell said.

"I'm not judging you in the least," McKenzie assured her.

"I'm judging me still. I hate that he was away from me for any time in the foster care system. When I finally got him back, at first I was overcompensating, barely letting him out of my sight. I was smothering him. But I was just so dang worried. But he's doing wonderfully now. He loves his school, and he's made such good friends. It kind of makes me sad how little he needs me now," she said with a sigh.

"You've done a great job with him. That shows you're an amazing sister, and I guess mom now, which is strange," McKenzie said.

"I'm just his sister, but I agree. It is certainly strange," Jewell said with a laugh.

"I think it's amazing," Blake said.

"I can't get used to this roses and butterflies attitude you now have," Byron said, but he laughed after.

"Don't worry, my brother, it won't be long until you have this same attitude," Blake assured him.

"Don't place any bets," Byron said, but then he sent McKenzie a look so intense she felt scorched in her seat.

Who was the real Byron? Was he the hard-ass she'd

first met? Or was he the kind brother-in-law and uncle? She really didn't know which man was an act and which one was genuine. The question was, though, did she want to know? The answer should be an emphatic no. But she wasn't so sure about that.

Once they finished dinner, Blake offered desert and coffee, but McKenzie knew she really should get home and get back to work. Why was she having such a tough time excusing herself?

"I have a ton of work to get done tonight, since I wasn't in the offices all day, so I'm going to have to pass," Byron said before McKenzie was able to make her own excuses. "Do you need a ride home, McKenzie?"

She felt caught. She couldn't exactly refuse him in front of Blake and Jewell, but the thought of being alone with him in his car sent tingles all through her body. That was trouble waiting to happen. Instead of saying *thanks but no thanks*, she found herself accepting, and before she knew it, the two of them had said their goodbyes and they were heading down the road.

McKenzie lived only about fifteen minutes from Jewell's place, and they made the drive in a silence she found excruciating. But for the life of her, she couldn't figure out a single thing to say to break the tension. Her vaunted social skills, honed at Relinquish Control, had completely deserted her.

When Byron pulled up in front of her house her stomach clenched. He got out while she was fumbling with her seatbelt and opened her door, then held out a hand to help her from the car.

Pretending not to see the hand, she climbed out, then went stiffly to her front door, inserted the key and twisted the knob. She turned around, waiting to see what Byron was going to do next.

"I had a wonderful time with you tonight. Thanks for sharing a dinner with me," Byron said, and then to her utter amazement, he walked back down her steps.

McKenzie stared after him, wondering what in the world was going on. There was no kiss, no prompting for her to invite him inside — nothing.

Now he was climbing into his car and starting the engine. She stepped inside, and looked out the window as he pulled out of her driveway. She stepped inside and shut her door, then looked out the window and watched his taillights fade away.

What had just happened?

Nothing. That's what had happened. Was Byron done with her? Was his game over? Had he lost his desire for her? Had her last refusal turned him away for good?

And, if it was all over, was that disappointment she was feeling?

Jewell didn't have a single answer to any of those questions.

CHAPTER SIXTEEN

A BEAD OF sweat dripped down McKenzie's temple as she walked alongside Byron. They'd just left the offices in Boise. Clouds covered the sky and rain threatened, but it was unusually warm, and she'd dressed for colder weather. It would have been much nicer to shrug off her jacket, but she felt more protected in her wool suit.

The two of them approached the rental car they'd picked up that morning upon landing at the Boise airport.

"I always hate it when I have to fire someone who's worked for the company for so long," Byron said as he unlocked the car and peeled off his jacket, setting it and his briefcase in the backseat.

"It's always troubling to fire anyone," she said as she climbed into the passenger side of the car and waited for him to climb in and start the engine so she could point the vent in her direction and cool off.

"At least when I threatened to close the entire operation down, we finally got some answers." He loosened his tie before pulling it off and tossing it over his shoulder into the backseat, and then he started the car.

She hated that his small stunt with the tie made her stomach clench with desire. He wasn't stripping for her; he was simply making himself more comfortable. But all she wanted to do at the moment was climb over the console and right into his lap.

It was Friday afternoon and nothing had happened between them since the dinner three days before. He'd come into work, behaved like a complete professional, and hadn't even attempted to touch her — shades of the way he'd left her on her front porch. And her job at Knight Construction was coming to a close. She only had a week to go. In the beginning the month had seemed like forever. Now, a week seemed so short.

She had her own business to run and didn't have time to be working on Byron's books, but in an amazingly short time she'd grown used to walking into his office in the morning when he was there, exchanging a few quick pleasantries with him, and speaking to him throughout the day.

When the man wasn't trying to intimidate her, he was actually pretty decent company. And the longer she was around him, the more she desired him. Was it because he wasn't doing anything lately to provoke that reaction?

But, hey, his loss of interest was the best thing that could have happened. He thought of her as a whore, so if she were to jump into bed with him, she'd be proving that's exactly what she was. And as her eyes traced the slight opening at the V of his neck, she knew she needed to get out of this car as soon as possible. She'd be fine as soon as they were back in Seattle, safe and sound, and miles away from each other. Yes, it was Friday. She'd have all weekend to pull herself together. And then only one week left with him.

Byron pulled out of the attached parking garage and they began rolling down the road. The air conditioning should have cooled her off, but her body was too heated for anything to have that effect. She was again tempted to ditch the jacket, but at this point, her blouse was slightly damp, and the last thing she wanted to expose was her lacy bra, so she'd just have to suffer in silence. They'd soon be at the airport. She'd rush to the bathroom and splash cold water on her face.

"I'm starving," Byron said, startling out of her train of thought. "Are you at all hungry?" he asked.

She tried to figure out exactly where they were, but she was about the most directionally challenged person around, so she stopped trying. "A little, but I can grab something at the airport." She didn't want to string this out any further.

"We have plenty of time, McKenzie."

His vague reply made her uneasy.

"What time is the flight?"

"We're taking a little side trip before heading home." He didn't elaborate, and McKenzie grew even more heated as nerves shot through her.

"What kind of side trip?" she asked. "And is it hot in here, or is it just me?" She reached over to fiddle with her vent again, feeling on the verge of fainting.

"It's not too warm," he said, a sparkle in his eyes that had her breathing even more heavily. He knew she was close to panic, and he also knew exactly what was making her that way.

"Side trip? Where?" Maybe if she talked with less words, he would answer.

"You'll see."

Ugh! She looked out her window and focused on breathing. Coming along on this trip had been a bad idea.

"I don't want to miss our flight," she finally said.

"McKenzie, I own the jet. It leaves when I'm ready, and you know that."

"Your brothers might need it," she pointed out.

"We have two of them. And if suddenly Blake and Tyler both need to go somewhere, it's only a one-hour flight back from here."

She really didn't have any more arguments for him, so she remained silent as he drove for another half an hour. He was moving farther and farther away from Boise, and she had a feeling they weren't going to be making the flight home tonight.

When they still weren't stopping, she had to say something or she was going to explode. "I'm not staying overnight with you, Byron." She really wished her words had come out with more oomph. But at least she'd managed to get them from her throat.

"Do you want to be more specific?" he asked, the weasel.

"We are *not* having sex." There. It didn't get more specific than that.

He was silent for a moment before he turned and looked at her for several heartbeats.

"Are you trying to convince me of this...or yourself?" he asked quietly.

"Look at the road!" she gasped, and he turned back forward.

It took a moment before she had anything to say to that, but then she decided to go on the offensive. "As one of the infamous Knight brothers, you're clearly used to getting women to jump into your bed, but I think you should know that I'm not a typical woman."

He laughed again. "I love what you must think of me," he told her. "But I'll promise you this — we won't do a single thing you don't want to do."

That didn't reassure her in the least.

CHAPTER SEVENTEEN

S ILENCE STRETCHED THICK and long in the car, and finally, McKenzie had no choice but to remove her jacket. She was going to pass out if she didn't. Even with the air blowing full blast on her face, she was sweating, uncomfortably hot.

"How hot it is out?" she gasped, grabbing her purse and pulling out a magazine she'd brought for the plane ride, fanning her face.

"Sixty-two degrees," Byron said with a knowing chuckle that had her grinding her teeth together.

"It must be the sun pouring in through the windows. It's magnifying the heat or something," she lamely said.

"Sure…" The word was drawn out, but she would choose to think that he believed her explanation.

When she next felt his fingers drift over her thigh and grip her hand, she jumped, her head spinning to look at him. She couldn't take his touch right now – anytime but right now.

When his thumb outlined the edges her knuckles,

before turning her hand around and tracing the inside of her wrist, she felt the touch all the way to her core, which was now pulsing and hot. She squeezed her thighs together and tried desperately to remember why she needed to pull her hand away – why she needed to stop this seduction right this minute.

With as much effort as she could possibly muster, she pulled her hand away and tucked it between her thighs, waiting for a supernova to come and just obliterate their car. It was so damn hot now, that could be the only explanation. It certainly *wasn't* her hormones.

After another ten minutes, she jumped when Byron reached over and squeezed her thigh. "Are you going to remain silent this entire ride?"

"How much longer is the ride going to be?" she countered.

"About thirty more minutes."

"Where are we going?"

"To one of my favorite places," he vaguely answered.

"That doesn't tell me anything," she said, but her lip turned up just the slightest bit. He was so excited, almost boyishly so, and it was hard for her not to appreciate the change in his demeanor. Even if he was kidnapping her.

"It's not a well known place, but I've been here before. It's a nice, small resort in the mountains. They have private cabins, while still having all the comforts of home, including room service," he said.

"Ah, we wouldn't want to go without room service," she said before turning to look at him, wishing she could make eye-contact. "How many cabins did you rent?"

Her stomach was nervous as she waited for his answer. "Two, but I'm hoping one of them remains empty," he said, and she let out the breath she'd been holding.

That he'd rented two meant a lot to her. Yes, he was obviously hoping for sex this weekend – it was the entire purpose of kidnapping her, but he was also giving her enough respect of offering her a separate sleeping quarter if she insisted on it.

"Considering that I want to pull this car off to a nice little logging road and strip your clothes off and touch every single inch of your silky skin right now, it may be a good idea for you to somehow distract me," Byron said, making her head whip around and look at him in partial shock and partial awe.

"Um…I don't…um…what do you want to talk about?" she finally managed to get out of her parched throat.

"Tell me about yourself. How did you end up in Seattle?"

That was a subject she really, really didn't want to talk about. "How about anything other than that?" she said, trying to make it a joke. He wasn't buying it.

"Everyone has a beginning, McKenzie, even if that beginning isn't what we think it should have been," he said.

"Why don't you tell me about your youth then?" she challenged. His shoulders tensed, but he didn't back away.

"I may do that, but you first."

She paused for a moment, because if there was something she knew definitively about Byron, it was that he didn't lie, and didn't make promises he wouldn't keep. He hadn't said he would tell her, but it was a big step for him to even consider it. It was enough that it loosened her tongue.

"I had a typical childhood when I was younger. Divorced parents, a sister…" She stopped as she choked on that word. She had begun the sentence as a joke, and already had revealed too much.

"Wait!" he said, his head whipping in her direction. "You have a sister?" he asked, his full attention on her.

"Please pay attention," she gasped when they swerved toward the ditch. He quickly corrected the wheel, then faced forward as he continued driving.

"Yes, I had a sister," she quietly said, not wanting to talk about it.

"Where is she? Why doesn't anyone know about her?" He obviously hadn't picked up on the word "had."

"When we were thirteen–"

Byron interrupted again. "We?" Of course he'd caught that.

"Susie and I are twins," she said quietly.

"I'm sorry. I won't interrupt again," he said before giving her a sheepish smile. "Or, I'll try really hard not to," he amended.

"When we were thirteen, my dad had given us a brand new quad. One of the nice things of being the children of divorce is when daddy comes to town, he's really trying to be the cool parent, so we always got really expensive, outrageous gifts that would drive our mother crazy. She told us we couldn't ride it until we were trained. Of course, she worked two jobs and couldn't exactly monitor us. We lived in a small town outside of Sacramento, up in the hills, and it was summer and we wanted to test out the new toy."

It hurt to even think about this day, let alone, relive it. She hadn't spoken about Susie in so long to anyone that her heart was aching tremendously. "Please go on, McKenzie," Byron said quietly.

"We took turns racing down some old logging roads, each of us fighting over who got to drive and who had to hang on for dear life. It was her turn to drive and she was all sorts of confident at this point. And our father, being who he was, had gotten us the toy but not the safety items needed with it. Neither of us had helmets."

McKenzie closed her eyes as she relived a brief second in time that had changed her life forever. "You can stop," Byron said, squeezing her thigh in reassurance. Yes, of course he thought he knew how this story was going to end.

"She didn't die," she whispered so softly she wasn't sure if Byron heard her or not.

"What?" he gasped, turning toward her again before realizing what he was doing and facing back forward.

"No, I felt guilt for years, because I wished she would have. It would have been better," she said.

"Tell me, McKenzie." It was a soft plea.

"We were going too fast and we came to a corner there was no way we could take at those speeds. We flew over the cliff and while still in the air, hit a tree," she said, a tear falling from her eye. "I blacked out immediately, but later they put all the pieces together and figured out what happened."

She took a few moments and composed herself before telling Byron something she hadn't told another living soul. How sad her life was that she had no one she could truly share with. No. She had Jewell now, but Jewell had a husband and responsibilities. It didn't matter. McKenzie wasn't normally the sharing type. She didn't understand why she was telling all of this to Byron – a man who most certainly didn't care about her at all.

Then again, maybe that's why she was sharing the story with him, because he didn't care and he would go away. Maybe it was sort of like talking to a therapist. She decided to continue.

"Susie's body protected mine because she flew forward, hitting her head on the tree, and cushioned my own impact. Her brain swelled and by the time help found us, I was awake, though I couldn't see, so I had no idea what bad shape Susie was in, let alone how to get out of the mess we were in. A family was out riding bicycles and found us, called emergency services and sat with us until they arrived. Susie went into a coma. She still hasn't come out. My mother..." She choked again, feeling the sting of her mother's words to the very depths of her soul.

"My mom was so distraught, she banned my father from coming near us again, and he was so consumed with guilt, he let her get away with it. And then, after she didn't have our father to yell at anymore, she turned her anger on me, telling me that she would still have her daughter if I hadn't been so reckless, hadn't been so much like our father, out to prove to the world how macho I was."

"McKenzie, those were just words spoken in grief," he said, which is what counselors had said to her before.

"Except that she never apologized, and then the longer she was in the care facility, the angrier she became. We lost everything – our house, possessions, everything, because Mom wouldn't leave her side, and the medical expenses were outrageous. After a year, she finally went back to work, but every dime she had went into Susie's care. My mother died when I was twenty, but not before telling me that I better take care of Susie, especially since I was the one responsible for the vegetable she had turned into.

Even on her dying breath, she was next to her, lying in a bed, holding her hand. She never gave up on praying that she would one day wake."

McKenzie had tears streaming down her cheek as she thought back to that day, thought back to those early years.

"What happened to her? How long was she in the coma?" he asked.

"Does that matter? Really? You don't give up on the people you're supposed to love," she said, wishing now she had never brought up this topic.

"McKenzie…" His voice was quiet.

"She died five months ago…" she barely managed to whisper.

It was the reason she'd sold Relinquish Control. She hadn't needed it anymore since she wasn't weighed down by huge medical bills. She could finally do what she wanted to do, and feeling that way sent a whole new level of guilt through her.

"I'm sorry," Byron said.

"That's what the doctors said, and the counselors. Everyone is always so sorry." She was still bitter, more bitter than she realized.

"McKenzie, your sister was in a coma for fifteen years," Byron said, not unkindly, but in a tone that ensured she would listen. Then the next words had her sobbing. "Would you have wanted to wake up after all that time and realize how many years had passed, that even though mentally you are a thirteen year old girl, physically you are twenty-eight, and the world expects you to act like it?"

No one had ever said those words to her – not a single person. She never had thought about what it would have been like for Susie to wake up and not know who she was, not even recognize herself in the mirror.

"I…I don't know. That's something I've never considered," she finally said.

"Your mother was wrong to keep her alive by machines and she was wrong to blame you. No matter who was driving, that's not the point, the point is, you were just being kids, having fun, and you both made a mistake – a tragic mistake, but still, a mistake," Byron pointed out.

"But I should have told her to slow down. I should have tried to grab the brake. And it was my responsibility to take care of her," she said, pulling away from him as she wrapped her arms across her chest. She'd been so hot for hours, and now she was unbearably cold.

"You did far more than what anyone could have expected of you. I think it's time for you to forgive yourself and your sister," he said as he pulled off the main road and took a long driveway that was flanked on either side with huge trees, creating a canopy, making her feel as if she were in a Southern movie.

"Well, we will just disagree," she said sadly.

"We *will* revisit this later. Right now, I want you to put away the sorrow and look ahead. We're here."

When they turned a corner, a beautiful three story building looked as if it was rising out of the mountain. "Home sweet home," she said, once again trying to make a joke, trying to push the sorrow away.

"Home sweet home," he repeated. He then stopped the car and turned toward her. "Do we need both cabins, McKenzie?"

CHAPTER EIGHTEEN

MCKENZIE SAT AT the bar and sipped leisurely on her martini. It was her second one, and she still didn't know what she wanted to do. No. That wasn't true. She knew exactly what she wanted to do. She wanted to let Byron take her to his cabin, slowly peel her clothes away, and make her forget everything bad in her life, make her feel something good. She had never thought sex would be a good experience, but for some reason, she knew it would be excellent with Byron. How she knew that, she would never know.

She took another sip and tried to form words, tried to tell Byron what she wanted. Nothing came from her throat — for some bizarre reason, it felt parched — so she sipped from her glass again.

What was wrong with her? This wasn't about love, or even about affection —far from it — but she knew what it was going into it, so what would be so wrong with discovering her body, with being a little selfish for the first time in a long while? Not that she expected complete satisfaction from any man.

Byron was handsome, devastatingly handsome, and she had no doubt that he would make her feel more sensations like the ones she felt when he kissed her. Sure, he had money, but she didn't care about that. It wasn't as if they were going to be a couple. This was about sex, and nothing more. She actually despised most men with money because they thought that they owned anything and everything they wanted because of it.

But this was so…so…clandestine, so forbidden. It was also very unusual for her. But, at the same time, she felt a certain amount of freedom in letting down her guard, in focusing on her needs. If only she could accept what he was offering, then she could be free of her worries.

After another half hour, he turned and looked at her. "What's it going to be, McKenzie? One bed…or two?"

* * *

Byron sat at the bar, inhaling McKenzie's sweet scent, feeling as if he wouldn't make it if she chose not to stay with him. Yes, he'd ambushed her with this place, and yes, he was pushing her, but he wasn't doing anything she didn't want to do.

She wanted to stay in his room. She wanted to let go. She just didn't want to admit that's what she wanted. She was stubborn, but what he didn't understand was why. Sex wasn't something new for her — the woman had been the madam of a very successful and very exclusive escort service.

Maybe this was her payback for the way he had approached her in the beginning. Yes, he knew she was a liar, and he knew she was out to get whatever she could get. But all women were like that. And though he never needed anyone, he somehow seemed to need her.

All he had to do was sleep with her — maybe one night, or maybe a few — and then he'd be able to begin purging her from his system. If he called a truce for a short time, she might give in, and give him his freedom.

Byron knew how to be romantic, how to put on a song and dance to impress a woman. It was just something he hadn't cared to do in a long while. If a woman weren't interested, then he would move on, because there would always be a line of eligible women waiting right behind each other — salivating over the chance that he would bed them.

No brag, just fact.

Was she was telling the truth about her sister? He wanted to believe it was just another lie in a long string of lies, but the pain in her voice, the sorrow in her eyes — that couldn't possibly be made up. Or could it?

He couldn't forget how well his mother had been able to lie. So he had to harden himself to McKenzie — no, no double entendre there. Yes, her story could well be all lies, something to soften him up… But this was something he could verify — if he cared enough to do so.

This whole trip, though, was obviously a fool's errand. She'd made her living by stringing men along, teasing them, keeping them panting for her wares. And if her sob story had a shred of truth in it, she might not be ready to accept what she needed and share his bed. Time to cut his losses, he decided.

Just then, her head turned. "Let's go to your cabin, Byron. I'd like to see it."

Byron could have sworn his heart stopped beating for a few seconds as she whispered those words. She'd set down her empty glass and was gazing at his throat. She refused to look him in the eyes.

He stood up like a flash and held out his hand. "This way," he said. He didn't want to give her a chance to change her mind.

They walked silently from the lobby bar and made their way down a small path to a large cabin, the lights welcoming, the heavy curtains keeping them from seeing inside until he opened the door and held out an arm for her to enter.

He'd been to this place before. It was a favorite retreat of his when he wanted to get away from the city, wanted time to think, wanted to be left alone. He'd never before brought a woman there — and that was something he definitely refused to analyze.

Though the cabin appeared rustic from the outside, the inside had all the modern conveniences that he was too spoiled to give up, and it boasted granite countertops, top-of-the-line stainless-steel appliances, hardwood floors, plush rugs, and a rock-faced fireplace with a stack of wood next to it.

This unit had only one bedroom, but two full-sized bathrooms, plenty of cupboards and drawers, and a decent-sized living room with a plush couch and a couple of overstuffed chairs.

"They even have books and magazines sitting out," McKenzie said as she slowly looked around the cabin.

"I hope you like it," he said, making sure his voice gave

nothing away — especially none of the anxiety he was suddenly feeling.

"It's beautiful." She turned toward the bedroom and he could see the tension in her eyes.

"I need a shower, McKenzie. I'll use the one out here in case you want to use the master bath."

Byron didn't give her a chance to say anything. Instead, he grabbed his bag, shut himself in the bathroom and took a second to lean against the door. What he should do was shower, walk from the bathroom naked, and ravish her.

It was what they both wanted, after all.

What he did was shower, shave and then get dressed. He'd promised her dinner. It would be better for both of them if they had some fuel inside them to sustain their nighttime activities.

When he came out, the cabin smelled of peaches, and he closed his eyes for a moment and inhaled, thinking he could get used to entering a room and having this experience over and over again.

Shaking his head with frustration, he pushed that thought out of his head. He was a loner, and preferred it that way. There was no need to change anything in his life. Just because he appreciated a woman who took care of herself didn't mean he needed to make a fool of himself over her.

He found McKenzie in the bedroom, looking in the mirror as she combed her wet hair. Their eyes connected in the mirror and she smiled what he would have thought was an innocent smile coming from anyone else. "The shower was heaven," she said with a nervous giggle as she set down the comb.

And Byron couldn't resist her any longer.

Taking a few short steps, he turned her around, and pulled her to him, bending and capturing her lips. He wanted her to know what she was missing by continuing to resist him, but after a single minute of his lips on hers, he wasn't sure any longer who was being taught a lesson.

His hands slid down her back, his palms cupping her sweet derrière, and he tugged, lining her hips up with his, letting her feel how hard he was now — how hard he was each time they were in a room alone together. Hell, they didn't even have to be alone. Since their first kiss, he always seemed ready in an instant to plunge into her sweet, hot folds.

When her soft sigh of surrender slipped into his mouth, he knew he could walk her backward, strip her clothes from her and thrust inside her. Somehow, knowing that helped to ease the pain he was feeling.

His lips softened as he gently traced her mouth with them, but he finally pulled back, triumph filling him at the desire shining in her eyes.

"We can finish what we've started, McKenzie, or I can feed you first, like I promised." Oh, how he hoped she'd take option one.

He could clearly see the conflict raging within her, and then he saw when she decided. Damn!

"I really am hungry," she croaked out, and the tremor in her voice made him feel much better about being rejected yet again.

"Then I will feed one hunger," he said before a big smile overtook his lips. "And then I'll feed the other."

She said nothing as he turned to leave, but he felt her follow him from the room and then from the cabin. As they strolled back toward the lodge, Byron found himself seeking McKenzie's hand. She didn't try to pull away from him as they walked along the trail.

He held the door for her as they entered the small restaurant, and they were soon seated on the back patio, deck heaters warming the area, the smell of pine trees filling the air.

"This is pretty amazing, Byron," she said with a sigh as she looked out into the dark gray of the night. The moon was nearly full, illuminating the hills, but there wasn't much of a view at this time of night.

"In the morning, this place is spectacular. I love sitting on the deck at the cabin, watching the sun come up, and hearing nothing but the sounds of the birds singing. Sometimes, I forget what it sounds like living in the city, where traffic drowns out any and all other sounds."

"That sounded slightly romantic, Byron. You'd better be careful what you say," she said with a sidelong glance under her full eyelashes and a smile that took his breath away.

"Well, then, we'd better look over the menu and figure out what we're going to eat. I wouldn't want to get too mushy and destroy my reputation," he said.

Though a reflex had made him instantly put up his defenses, something inside him resisted it. He wanted to be a different person this weekend, wanted to speak of sunrises and sunset, and birds singing. But that wasn't who he was. That wasn't what this was about. It was about sex, and nothing but sex. And if he weren't careful, Byron would get a lot more than he was bargaining for, and that wasn't something he was willing to accept.

No. It was much better to focus on sex and pleasure, and it was much better for him to remember exactly who

McKenzie Beaumont was. She used to run a bordello. She certainly wasn't the innocent face she was trying to show him and the rest of the world right now.

Byron tried making idle chitchat for a few minutes. But their waiter came, took their order, and brought bread and drinks, and the conversation died out. Soon he was lost in his own head while their meal was served, and they ate in silence.

When they finished, he signed the check, then found himself taking her hand again as they made their way back to the cabin. His heart pounded as they drew near, and he felt the nervous tension in her body, but he was done with all the games.

They'd come to this place to discover each other. And that's exactly what they were going to do. The moon cast a glow over their walk back, the breeze cool enough to keep her locked tightly to his side.

When they arrived back at the cabin, Byron stopped after he opened the door. He looked down, gazing into her eyes. He wanted no doubt in her mind about what was going to happen the second they stepped over the threshold.

"If you don't want this, we need to part ways right now," he warned her, lifting his hand and letting it trail through her hair.

"Wh…what do you mean?" she stuttered, a shiver traveling through her.

"You know exactly what I mean," he said, his voice firming the slightest bit from the restraint it was taking him to say this. "The cabin right next door is mine, too. Tell me no right now, and I'll leave you here and we'll both have a very unsatisfying night."

Her face blanched just a little, and he could see that she didn't want to say the words. She wanted him to take the choice from her. He wasn't going to show her that kindness. He wanted her to admit how much she wanted him.

Still, he held his breath, afraid that she would refuse, that she would deny them both. But he pushed that fear aside. She was his for the taking — she just needed to say the words.

His heart stalled as her lips opened and he waited for her final verdict.

CHAPTER NINETEEN

Y ES."
She couldn't say anything other than the one word she needed to say or fear dying right there on the front porch of this cabin in the woods of Idaho.

Byron's eyes widened just a bit, and she could see raw need practically vibrating off him. It gave her the confidence of knowing she was making the right choice — at least, the right choice for now.

It was obvious when the last of Byron's patience broke. He grabbed her hand, dragging her across the threshold of the cabin, and without another word, he pulled her into his arms. After he kicked the door shut, his mouth captured hers in a hungry kiss.

Yes, she needed this man. No more worries flitted through her brain as his mouth and hands stoked the fire building up within her. Could something that felt this right ever be wrong? No way.

She threaded her fingers through his hair as her body arched into his, and she rubbed her aching core against his straining erection, desperate for their clothes to disappear. "I need you," she whispered huskily when he released her lips so he could trail his tongue down the side of her throat.

"I've been wanting to hear those words for a while now," he growled before lifting her into his arms. He carried her to the bedroom and set her down gently beside the bed.

Her skin was on fire as he began removing her clothing, kissing each new area of skin as he exposed it. When he dropped to his knees, pulling her jeans down with his hands and trailing his lips across her thighs as he exposed them, she trembled before him, barely able to keep from falling backward.

His mouth came back up, and his tongue slid along her thigh before moving upward and gliding across her stomach. Her knees couldn't take it anymore, and they gave out, sending her sliding backward onto the luxurious bed behind her.

"Mmm, are you feeling weak, McKenzie?" he asked with a husky chuckle. Before she could reply, he began removing his own clothes, and her throat tightened at the male beauty before her.

Perfection.

He was pure, unadulterated perfection, and she found herself wanting to trail her tongue along his skin like he had done with her. "You're taking too long," she gasped, making his fingers stall as he looked at her with such fire, she didn't know how she wasn't burned.

He quickly shed the rest of his clothes, grabbing several condoms from his pocket before tossing his pants aside. He climbed onto the bed with her and immediately drew her into his arms.

Skin to skin had never felt so right. She arched into him, loving the feel of his hard planes against her soft curves. They were a perfect fit. She knew they'd fit in every way possible. She knew this was right.

"Pure silk," he murmured as his lips glided across her collar bone before moving down to caress the tops of her breasts. She gasped as his tongue circled her peaked nipple before he sucked it into his mouth, making her arch off the mattress and grab his head to hold him right where he was. "And greedy," he murmured, pulling away from her just long enough to speak, then diving right back in and sucking her aching body.

When he crawled back up her body and turned her on her side to face him, she finally had the chance to explore him. Her hands seemed so small as she splayed them on his tanned skin. She pushed him onto his back and took her time kissing the salty muskiness of his neck before moving down and flicking her tongue across his exquisite pecs.

"So hard," she murmured as she reached his stomach, her hands preceding her to his thighs, and the beauty that lay between them. "So solid…" Her words were a reverent whisper as her hand circled his throbbing manhood.

Not hesitating in the slightest, she leaned down and tasted his satin head, its salty flavor exploding in her mouth.

"McKenzie… I'm too close to embarrassing myself for you to do that," he groaned, and he reached hands into her hair and tugged.

She ignored him and let her mouth sink down deeper onto his thickness while her fingers gripped him tightly. "Mmmm…" she moaned, the sound muted by his flesh filling her mouth.

"Enough!" He sat up and pulled her head off him, and then flipped her onto her back and covered her body with his. The pure heaven of feeling his manhood resting along the seam of her core made her whimper. He slid his hands beneath her and tugged her hips upward while he rubbed along the outside of her heat, soaking his erection with her arousal.

She reached for him, needing to guide him inside her, but he gave her a look of victory as he pulled his hands from beneath her and grasped her wrists, then pinned them above her head, trapping her beneath him.

"Take me now, Byron," she begged, but he just leaned down and kissed her again, silencing her in the most efficient way.

Spreading her thighs wider, she bent her knees and pushed against him, wriggling beneath his solid form as she tried to force him to enter her.

"You are enough to test a saint," he groaned as the tip of his erection slid a couple of inches inside her heat.

"Then take me, damn you," she told him. "We've both suffered enough." She, pushed upward again, desperate to have all of him.

He pulled back and she whimpered in protest. This game of his wasn't to her liking. She was ready to feel pleasure, and he was holding back. Her eyes narrowed as she tried to pull her hands free.

He released his hold and she immediately wound her fingers in his hair and pulled his mouth back to hers. She devoured his lips, slipping her tongue inside his mouth and capturing his hungry groan.

But before she could pull him inside her, he pulled

those precious couple of inches out of her then released her mouth, and trailed his lips down her body again, this time making a beeline to the part of her that ached the most.

When his mouth circled her core and he swiped his tongue across her painfully swollen bud, she felt her release coming. Within seconds he had her crying out as her body shook in ecstasy. And then the room darkened as her body clenched repeatedly in what seemed a never-ending paroxysm of bliss. So, this was what sex was all about. Now, she understood how she'd made so much money over the years.

"Now you're ready, McKenzie."

She opened her eyes to find him poised above her, and then with one solid push, he thrust inside her wet heat, making her cry out.

The air whooshed out of her lungs as he paused, his entire length buried within in, her walls still pulsing with the pleasure of her orgasm. She'd never felt anything like this before.

"How are you so tight?" he groaned. But she didn't want to talk. She wanted to feel more pleasure.

She moved her hips upward, needing him to plunge in and out of her. He placed a hand on her hip and held her in place. "Wait," he groaned as his eyes closed and his head leaned back, a look of utter pleasure filling his face.

Finally, he began moving, pulling his hardness almost completely from her before he pushed back hard inside, rocking her entire body. This time, they both groaned together at the pure pleasure of the movement.

Barely before her first orgasm ended, she felt an immediate pressure build again, and her eyes widened as she looked into Byron's eyes, his narrowed as he began moving faster, filling her over and over again.

Then he leaned down and captured her lips as he grabbed her hip and drove hard and fast within her needy body. A cry was wrenched from her and he took it greedily as she began convulsing around him, an orgasm even more intense than her first.

He thrust inside her again, and then once more, before his body tensed and he buried his mouth into the curve of her neck, his loud groans vibrating against her skin as she felt him pulse inside her.

After an endless amount of time, Byron's body sank against her, their skin hot and slick, their breathing shallow, their initial hunger sated.

"I've never…," she began to say before letting her words trail off. She couldn't tell him that.

"You've never what, McKenzie?" he asked against her ear, his tongue tracing the outline and making her shiver.

"Nothing," she murmured. She couldn't believe the way her body was responding to his tongue.

"I have ways of making you talk," he said. His mouth returned to her neck and started sucking on the tender skin there.

"And I have ways of making you forget to question me," she warned, her hands sliding down his back and over the firm muscles of his buttocks.

"Witch," he said so quietly she wondered if she'd heard him right.

But she felt a twitch from his still buried erection, and then she felt him begin to move again. All talking was forgotten as he began making love to her once more.

She was terrified. This was something she could get all

too used to.

CHAPTER TWENTY

TWO NIGHTS AND one full day of pretty much nothing except for making love. In the bed, in the shower, on the small kitchen table, the couch, in front of the fire and more… Byron was pretty certain they had christened every square inch of the cabin.

Yet still he stood on the front porch, watching the soft morning sunrise, and he wasn't sated. He wanted more. He couldn't remember a time when he'd spent so much time with one woman, made love so many times, and still felt unsatisfied.

Not that he wasn't pleasured beyond his wildest imagination each and every time. But as soon as they were finished, he could take her again, and again, and again… He was beginning to wonder whether he'd ever get enough of this small but surprisingly strong woman.

If he didn't get himself under control soon, he would be no better than his pathetic father. Is this what had happened to his dad? Had the man been so infatuated with Byron's mother that, after she had control over his body, she had been able to destroy him? It seemed a very likely conclusion to make from the way things had ended with his parents.

Sex was essential to survival. It might not be listed as one of the food groups, but it certainly should be. But even so, a myriad of women were ready and waiting to offer the use of their bodies. There was no reason a man should ever lock himself down with just one.

Okay, the thought of making love with any woman other than McKenzie turned his stomach. But that was something he would have to change. Maybe he needed to just cut this off, to push her out of his life, at least if he wanted to keep his sanity intact. He didn't need answers to who she was. Screw all the mystery.

It was settled, then. He was going to fly McKenzie back home, release her from her contract with him, and never see her again.

Even though she was friends with his sister-in-law, he could easily avoid her. But just the thought of acting that way infuriated him. Since when did he, Byron Knight, ever need to hide from anything or anyone? He hadn't done it since he was a child and witnessed the gruesome murder of his parents. That day had hardened him, and he was determined to stay hard.

As he shifted uncomfortably on the front porch, he realized he was already hard in other ways. They had last made love only a few hours before, and it was taking every ounce of strength within him not to march into the cabin and wake her by sinking deep within her tight body. And how could a madam be so tight? He'd barely fit inside her the first time.

There was so much that didn't fit when it came to

McKenzie. And the entire point of this weekend had been to exorcise her from his system, not find more questions he feared he would not ever receive answers to. He'd planned on satisfying his body's needs first, and then interrogating her.

He'd never gotten around to the interrogation part.

He had to stay focused, to remember who and what she was. She had messed in the life of his brother. And if a person messed with one of the brothers, then they messed with all of them.

Tyler and Blake were the only blood he had, the only true friends he had, the only two people on the planet he would take a bullet for. Oh, wait. There was also Justin, so Byron guessed it wasn't only the three of them anymore. He now had a nephew, and soon another niece or nephew.

No matter how hard he tried to resist opening his heart, he was being forced against his will to do so. He hadn't wanted to like Justin, not at all. He was an interloper. But how could he not adore the small boy with so much strength? The kid reminded him a lot of his brother, even though his brother hadn't known of the boy's existence until last year.

Why did everything have to change? Why couldn't they have just gone through their lives with no bumps in the road? His eyes narrowed. Because Blake had met McKenzie Beaumont.

The creaking of the door alerted him to the fact that he was no longer alone, but even without it, he would have known. Though he sure as hell didn't want to, Byron had a sense of when McKenzie was around. He felt her presence.

But it didn't fill him with anger. Instead, the feel of her satin-encased arms wrapping around his back brought peace to his thoughts. Her open hands slid beneath his shirt and caressed the skin of his stomach as she leaned into his back.

"Morning," she mumbled.

The raspy sound of her sleepy voice sent lust surging through him. Closing his eyes, he took a deep breath as he tried to tamp down his desire.

"You're up a lot earlier than I thought you'd be," he said. Almost against his will, his hands lifted to settle over hers, and his fingers caressed her soft skin.

"I woke up cold without you lying there," she whispered.

Her words should again have sent terror through him, or anger, or anything other than an odd sense of joy. He didn't want her to get used to him being there. This was all temporary, and though she'd said she knew the score here, she was getting too familiar already.

So why wasn't he pushing her away?

"I have an obligatory party I'm attending next Friday. You will come with me," he found himself saying. Huh? Yep, he'd called it right. Insanity.

Her hands stilled on his skin and her body tensed the slightest bit, before he felt her take a breath and relax. She resumed caressing his skin, but he could feel the tension inside her.

"I would rather not." He waited, but she didn't elaborate.

Turning, he leaned against the rail of the porch and tugged her into his arms, needing to look in her eyes, to see what she was trying to hide.

"I want you to be there." If he wanted it, then she should know that's exactly what he would get.

"No, you don't. I'm not good with parties, and I'm sure you have a list of people willing to go with you."

Anger flashed through him again. She was right. That was far too much like a date, and they weren't dating. They weren't boyfriend and girlfriend. They weren't anything to each other. He should be grateful she was refusing him.

So why wasn't he?

"I know what I want. If I said I want you there, then I want you there," he said, a dangerous edge to his voice.

She was quiet for a moment as she looked at him. "We both know what we're doing, Byron. Don't try to make it something it's not." She spoke with a smile, but he knew she wasn't kidding.

Before he could make a response, a wicked gleam lit her eyes, and she pulled from his grasp, then dropped to her knees, and reached inside the sweats he wore. She pulled him free, and the cool air didn't affect his hardness at all. No shrinkage.

"What are you doing, McKenzie? People could be walking by," he said, turning to look out at the trail, which was only a few hundred yards from their cabin.

"Then you'd better shield me," she said before taking him in her mouth and making him forget everything they'd been talking about.

Within minutes, Byron felt his release coming. "Stop now," he groaned, but his fingers were tangled in her hair.

His words only served to spur her on and speed her up, and he barely managed to muffle his cry as he spilled his seed inside the warm recesses of her mouth. After he stopped shaking, he pulled her back up into his arms, covering himself as he again tried to figure out what the hell she was doing to him.

"Your turn," he said, and he lifted her into his arms and carried her inside the cabin. But before he stopped speaking altogether, he delivered this warning: "You've only managed to delay this conversation, McKenzie. You *will* agree to go to the party with me."

Maybe later, when he wasn't in a sexual haze, he might realize what a dangerous road he was taking while he explored his infatuation with one McKenzie Beaumont.

CHAPTER TWENTY-ONE

I T'S A GOOD thing I don't spend every weekend like that one," McKenzie said as they approached her house, a yawn slipping from her before she was able to stop it.

"I thought it was a pretty great weekend," Byron said. He seemed offended somehow.

This was how he'd been behaving since they'd left the cabin in Idaho, though — grumpy and more like the man she had first met than the man who'd let down his guard for a couple of blissful days.

"It's not that I didn't have an amazing time. It's just that I need sleep. Most humans do, you know," she said with a false laugh. The closer they got to her house, the more downcast she felt. Their time was just about up.

She had managed to distract him from his discussion of next Friday's party, but only because she knew he would regret inviting her the minute they separated. He was on a sex high right now, but McKenzie had no illusions about where she stood with Byron Knight.

They were consenting adults, they'd had great sex, and now it was done. They weren't a couple, never would be a couple, and it was something she needed to keep reminding herself of. Yes, they'd managed to spend a couple of days together without the walls caving in around them, but that didn't in any way mean that they were compatible.

Anyone could have sex. It was how the species survived. But men like Byron Knight didn't settle down, and if they did, it certainly wasn't with women like McKenzie. He would never look past the fact that she'd owned an escort service. He was an important businessman, and she was just dipping her toes in the waters of what she considered the legitimate business world.

She needed to appreciate the good weekend, finish her time at Knight Construction, and then get on with her life. The last thing she needed to do was go on a real date with Byron. That would put ideas in her head — ideas she shouldn't be considering if she cared for her mental health.

After pulling into her driveway, Byron shut off his car and turned to face her. "Invite me in, McKenzie." The intensity in his voice nearly made her issue that invitation.

At the last minute she managed to keep her mouth shut as she tried to form the right words. "We both know that's not a good idea. I invite you in, we head straight to my bedroom. We had our weekend, Byron. It's now time for us to go back to our real lives," she said as she undid her seat belt.

She had to get away from this man — the sooner, the better.

"You know that you aren't ready for this weekend to end," he said, reaching over and cupping her neck before she could exit the car. "Your body knows what I can give it, so stop fighting me every step of the way." That sounded like a command.

"My body — along with every other part of me, including my muddled brain — is exhausted," she replied, only partially joking.

He paused before a beautiful smile filled his sensuous mouth. "Then we will just have dinner — no sex," he said, looking at her as innocently as he possibly could.

Though she knew she should say no to him, she found herself nodding. He was right. She wasn't ready for their weekend to end. It didn't count as a date when it was still Sunday and they hadn't parted yet.

Even she had to scoff inwardly at that absurd rationalization for spending more time with him now that they were back home. She knew that the more she prolonged this, the more it was going to batter her fragile heart. But knowing what was best and acting accordingly were two entirely different things.

"Wait," he told her as he got out of the car. She was shocked when he came to the passenger side and opened her door. Byron never professed to be a gentleman; so what was he doing now?

"Thank you," she said quietly, then waited while he grabbed her bag from his trunk.

They only made it a few feet when McKenzie froze in her driveway. Byron wasn't expecting her to stop, and he bumped into her. "What's the matter?"

She didn't have to tell him. He turned his head and saw the same thing she did. Humiliation burned through her, and McKenzie found herself fighting tears as she stood next to Byron, the humiliation so much worse with him as a witness.

"Call the police now," he said though clenched teeth.

"There's nothing they can do about this," she said with a sad shake of her head.

"That's bullshit, McKenzie. This is vandalism and defamation of character," he thundered.

"Please calm down, Byron. I don't need the neighbors alerted to what's going on," she said as she looked around. Her embarrassment was already too high, so she didn't need it to get worse.

"Really? That's what you're concerned with right now? What your neighbors think?" he fired off.

"Yes. Maybe you don't give a damn what people think of you, but I do," she snapped as she turned from the car and marched up her porch steps. She was on a mission to find sandpaper, spray paint, anything that would erase what had been done.

Byron caught up to her before she was able to unlock the front door. "Maybe someone saw something, saw who did this," he said.

"I doubt it," she said, and she got out her keys and opened the door.

"Dammit, McKenzie, something needs to happen!"

"Why, Byron?" she shouted as they entered her house. Her humiliation, her exhaustion, her stress all reached a peak. "You call me the same thing. So why in the hell do you even care?"

He took a step back as if she'd slapped him. "I would never spray-paint the word *whore* across your vehicle," he finally whispered.

"What's the difference between painting it on my car and calling me one?"

"McKenzie...," he began, but she held up a hand to stop him.

She didn't need to hear him try to explain himself. She knew who he was. She knew who she was. And they would never find common ground.

"Just go home, Byron. I need to get this fixed," she told him, so tired she suddenly couldn't even see straight.

His shoulders stiffened as he looked at her. "What in the hell aren't you telling me? I know there are problems in your life, and this just cements it. Why don't you let me help you?"

"Nothing is going on, Byron. It was probably drunk teenagers thinking they are being funny, and my house was empty so they went on the attack. It was just my car that they harmed."

Without asking for her permission, Byron pulled out his phone, dialed, and soon arranged to have her car picked up and taken in for repairs. She would have tried to stop him, but she was learning to choose her battles. And the reality was that she needed her car and she simply didn't have the emotional stamina left to deal with the problem right then.

When he hung up the phone, she moved into her living room and sat down. She had told him he could stay for dinner, but she didn't have the energy to prepare it, and she wanted more than anything for Byron to just pull her into his arms and take care of her. That angered her. She wasn't weak, and that was such a weak thing to want.

Byron followed her, a look of concentration on his face, as if he were trying to find the right words to say. She had no idea what was going to come next.

"Go and gather some clothes. I'll bring you to my

house."

She waited for him to continue, but he didn't say anything else. She closed her eyes for a brief second as she fought the desire to do just that. But there was no way she could accept his offer. If she did, then she would certainly become reliant on Byron and that was as dangerous as facing whoever had damaged her property. Maybe even more dangerous.

"I think our weekend is over now, Byron," she finally said, crossing her arms against her chest.

"What is that supposed to mean?" He took a step closer to her.

"I'm not coming to your house, and I'm too tired to cook. I think you should leave." That was pretty cut-and-dried, though it was killing her to say it.

"What if whoever did that comes back?" he asked. "You aren't safe here." He began pacing her small living room, making it seem even smaller than normal.

"I've been taking care of myself for a long time, and I don't need to start leaning on anyone now," she almost growled. She was too close to falling apart right now. If he touched her, she would completely lose it.

"I want to… Look, McKenzie. Just let me take care of you."

McKenzie froze. She had no idea what Byron meant by that, but she was sure it wasn't what she needed it to mean. How could he take care of her when he thought she was so horrible?

He couldn't.

"Look, Byron, this weekend was a bad idea. Sure, the sex was great, but now that we're back here, I realize that it…um…complicates things. I need to just finish my job, and you need to go back to doing whatever it is you do. There's no reason for this game to continue. We've already had sex," she said with a humorless laugh. "I'd really prefer it if you left now. This has to end here."

His face went blank, and he stopped and stared at her for several tense heartbeats. "Are you sure that's what you want?"

No! That wasn't what she wanted at all, but it was what she needed to happen. What she wanted was for him to take her in his arms and tell her the world was right and that she would never hurt again. What she wanted was for him to want her for more than just a good time in the closest bed. But that's not what she could tell him.

"Yes. It's what I want."

He moved over to the couch and leaned down, resting his weight against the back as he came within inches of her face. "Be very sure that's what you want, McKenzie. Because I don't need to be told no over and over again. I wanted you; I pursued you. We had sex. If you really want me to go away, I will walk out your door and never come through it again," he warned her, his hot breath caressing her face.

She waited until she was sure her voice wouldn't shake when she spoke, and then she was proud that she wasn't so choked up that the welling tears would come through in her words. "Would you like me to find a replacement tomorrow? I have two people who are more than ready to take my place at your company."

His eyes narrowed and he leaned a half an inch closer before pushing back to put a distance of several feet between them. She had a feeling he'd done it to keep himself from putting his hands around her throat and squeezing. But she'd never know for sure.

"No. Be at work tomorrow. I'll send a driver."

With that, he turned and walked from her house. She heard him start the car, heard him pull away, and still she sat there as still as a statue. It was at least fifteen minutes before she managed to stand up and look out her window to verify that he was indeed gone. Then, and only then, did she curl up in a ball on her couch and let the tears fall.

All she had truly wanted was for him to wrap her in his arms. But she hadn't been brave enough to ask him. And now it didn't matter anyway. He was gone.

CHAPTER TWENTY-TWO

BYRON WAS FURIOUS. He'd had to get away from McKenzie's house before he did something he might have regretted later. Not that he ever allowed himself to feel regret. That was for the weak, and Byron wasn't a weak person.

He was trying to help McKenzie against all odds, and she'd had the nerve to throw it back in his face. How dare she! This wasn't the first time she'd refused his kind offer. Why did he keep doing it? It made no freaking sense. She didn't deserve his help, not with the kind of person she was.

But the two of them had enjoyed a great weekend together. Not that they should have. And he was to blame. He'd pushed it. And how he had pushed… Damn! He hadn't felt this confused since he was a child. He didn't like it one little bit.

He should have taken her up on her suggestion that she leave Knight Construction. He should say goodbye to this woman and never look back. Dammit! Even the thought of doing that turned his guts inside out. What in the hell was going on with him?

He slammed his fist against the steering wheel while he was stopped at a red light. When a car behind him honked, he realized that the light had turned green and he was still sitting there. Slamming his foot against the gas pedal, he peeled away from the intersection with a mighty squeal and made his way toward home.

He and McKenzie were nothing to each other. They weren't even friends, or even lovers. They had shared a casual weekend of sex, but that didn't put them in a "relationship," and he shouldn't give a damn if something was going on in her life that was causing her distress.

But as much as he tried to convince himself, he couldn't help but worry, couldn't help but want to step in and live up to his last name. It was ridiculous of him because he was one of the people in line who wanted her destroyed — or at least he had been one of the people in line.

He tried to assure himself that as soon as her life wasn't in danger — if it even was —he would be able to send her away without a second thought. He had wanted to mess with her the way she'd messed with his brother. But now the victory he thought he would feel over breaking her was leaving a bitter taste in his mouth.

He wasn't certain how he'd made it home; he sure as hell wasn't concentrating on his driving. But there he was, and he parked and went inside. The change of scenery didn't change the tenor of his thoughts, however. He really needed to just let this go. But no matter how many times he tried to convince himself of just that, he couldn't do it, couldn't lift his phone and tell her not to come into work, that she could go back to her accounting business, free and clear, with a great reference from him for a job well done.

As Byron lay in bed that night, he told himself it was only because he hadn't extinguished the need he felt for her. A few more times in his bed and he would have his fill and send her on her way. Without her there, however, he spent a restless night tossing and turning, the little sleep he managed to get marred by nightmares with McKenzie drifting away.

So when he walked into his building the next morning, he was exhausted, and more of a bear than usual. At least his team of employees knew him well enough to read the look on his face. Not one person tried to speak to him as he stormed past to his office.

They knew it was best for all concerned if they let him be.

Byron sat at his desk and attempted to get down to some actual work, or at least to look as if he were doing so. After ten minutes of this wasted effort, he gave up and stood. He needed to know that McKenzie was next door, right where he'd told her to be.

Standing in her doorway, he felt his spirits lift slightly when he saw the exhaustion lining McKenzie's face — her night hadn't been any better than his. Had she missed him the night before as much as he had missed her? What other reason could there be?

Then he remembered one, and worry set back in.

What if someone had come back to her house? No. She was sitting in the offices. She was fine. Or maybe she wasn't. Anyone would be rattled by the events of the day before. She certainly had real emotions. Maybe he just wanted those dark circles to mean she had missed him.

"The driver I sent for you said you weren't there," Byron

remarked.

She looked up, but by the expression showing on her face, she'd already been aware he was there. He knew the feeling. She simply had to be nearby and he could feel her presence.

"I took a cab to work. I told you I don't need your help," she said, her voice devoid of emotion.

"Dammit, McKenzie! I'm losing my patience with you," he snapped as he stepped into her office and shut and locked the door.

Her face blanched, and she sat back, eyeing him warily. "I'm sorry. As I said, I shouldn't work here anymore, Byron."

"What you should do is tell me what in the hell is going on." He toned down his anger, but he wasn't leaving this office until he got some sort of answer from her.

"I don't trust people," she finally told him, her eyes filling with tears.

"Why not?" He waited.

Her tears evaporated, and she gave him a stubborn look. "It doesn't matter, Byron, but I know better than to rely on anyone but myself."

"You can't do your job if you are holding this much stress inside, McKenzie. The best thing you can do is tell someone." He took a chair and set it next to hers, making her face him.

"I can do my job just fine. Work is what keeps me focused," she said.

"Look, I'd be happy if I didn't give a damn about you. I'm trying not to. But we have…something going on between us. I need to know what is happening in your life." Byron immediately wanted to take those words back, but they were out there, so he sealed his lips together and waited.

"Don't waste your time feeling anything for me, Byron. My life is messed up, and you know that only too well. We'd be nothing but trouble together," she said with a bitter laugh.

"I have never told any other woman anything remotely close to what I just said to you. Don't make me regret it." He grabbed her hand and rubbed his thumb on the delicate skin of her palm. She inhaled deeply and tugged on her hand, but he refused to loosen his grip. "Talk to me," he demanded.

Her lips parted but nothing came out of her mouth. She took another breath, then looked away from him for several moments, focusing her eyes out the window. He waited.

Still she said nothing to him, and short of violence he didn't know how to get through to her. Really, he didn't need to do this to himself. "I'm trying to be a decent guy, and you're pushing me away," he finally said.

Silence again ensued for so long that he wondered if she was going to speak to him at all. Then she turned and looked at him, so much sadness in her expression that it shook him to his core, making him wonder if he'd gotten anything at all right about her.

"I just want to get back to work," she finally said, defeat coming through loud and clear.

"Then work it is…for today."

He left her office. Byron had a lot to think about — a lot of things he didn't want to think about. He had no idea where this was going with McKenzie, but he knew one thing for sure: the surprises weren't over. She was getting closer and closer to talking to him. She eventually would.

CHAPTER TWENTY-THREE

MCKENZIE WAS STILL sitting motionless at her desk fifteen minutes later. Just the thought of working seemed insurmountable; forget about actually doing the work. She had been so close to speaking with Byron, to sharing everything with him, but she knew that would be a monumental mistake. Men like him couldn't be trusted – hell, very few men actually could.

She didn't trust him or his motives, and she suspected that he was trying to gather evidence or something like that to use against her. She'd be a fool to forget that, to open her life and her heart to that man. And she'd been a fool one too many times already.

She picked up her cooled-off coffee and took a drink. She didn't even care that it tasted like crap. She was only in it — or vice versa —for the caffeine.

She kept giving herself mental slaps to wake herself up. She couldn't allow herself to think for even a single second that she and Byron had really shared anything together the last few days. They'd spent a weekend having sex. It had been beyond her wildest imagination good sex, but still just sex. If she imagined it to be anything other than that, she was a fool. She'd been deceived before, and she damn well wasn't going to let it happen again.

The temptation to lean on him, though, was killing her.

But enough of this. Putting aside her personal problems and worries, McKenzie forced herself to get back to work. After about an hour, she was doing okay with that — no, she wasn't moving as quickly or as efficiently as she thought she should be moving, but she was at least getting something done. Something other than moaning and groaning about a past that was over, that is.

When her phone rang just before lunch, she looked down and smiled. She hadn't spoken with Zach since last Thursday and she was actually missing the guy.

"Good morning, Zach. How are things over there?"

"Without you, my love? Without you here, they can't be better than okay."

"Oh, no. Is there something wrong?"

Zach chortled. "No. Of course not. Hard as it may be to believe, I'm capable of doing my job."

"Then why in the world are you trying to scare me?" she demanded.

"I wasn't. I was trying to let you know that this place will never be the same without you here," he told her. "I forgot for a moment how you can go from point A to point Z in one second flat."

"I'm just ready to get back in there. I can only do this freaking job for so long before I go completely insane."

"Are things any better there between you and Byron?"

"I shouldn't have told you he is a pain in my ass," she

said. "But…yes, they're just fine — pretty much the same," she lied.

"Okay, McKenzie, keep things to yourself. I'll try not to be too offended," he told her with an elaborate sigh and a slight sniff.

"And you can quit being so dramatic, Zach."

"Well, I was just calling to let you know that the accountant you're filling in for contacted us today," he said.

"What are you talking about?"

"Remember why you're there? The head accountant who met with an unfortunate accident? The guy, Norm Dannon, called us this morning to let us know that he wouldn't be able to return to Knight Construction. Effects of the accident and all that. So you'll need to find someone who can take your place, 'cause if you plan to stay there permanently, our business is going to go down in flames. Or up in smoke. Or…never mind."

She paused for a second as his words processed. "Why in the world is he calling you?"

"There was a mix-up in communication. He called in to personnel and they directed him to our number for some reason. I told him he'd best call them back, but I just wanted to give you a heads up."

McKenzie was instantly irritated. Did Byron already know about this? Had he been trying to keep it from her? She doubted she'd get the answers even if she did try to talk to him about it.

"Thanks, Zach. And I promise I won't be here very much longer."

"I see you're on the phone again." Byron's irritated voice interrupted her call.

McKenzie looked up to find him standing in her

doorway, looking less than pleased.

"I'll talk with you later, Zach. See you very soon," she told him, looking directly into Byron's eyes as she said it. Then she hung up the phone.

"What do you mean by that, McKenzie?" Byron asked her as he came closer.

She decided to answer a question with a question. "Did you know that Norm wasn't coming back?"

He didn't respond immediately, and as always she couldn't tell what he was thinking, because he blanked his expression. She really wished she could do that as well as him. She would pay just about every last dime of her precious savings to know what was going on behind that mask.

"Yes. I was going to inform you today. I've decided to hire Mary to replace him."

This was what McKenzie wanted, so she didn't understand the sudden sadness that was creeping through her. There was no way she would allow that to show on her face, though. Not a chance.

"That's wonderful. I can tell her right away, if you'd like, and get her in here and up to speed." She was speaking as stiffly right now as he'd just been.

"That won't be necessary. I'll have our human resources people set her up in an office here and go over everything. She was very capable. It won't take long for her to catch on."

McKenzie was stunned. This man had been plunging in and out of her body at this same time the day before, and now he looked so cool, so professional…so indifferent. It was more than obvious that he'd gotten what he wanted, and now he was more than ready to be rid of her.

She smiled brightly. "That's wonderful. Then I guess I'll clean up my stuff and head out of here," she said, trying to infuse some excitement into her tone.

"Thank you for filling in, McKenzie."

And then he turned and walked from her office.

Yes, her time with Byron was truly over. As quickly as it had begun, it had ended. She sat there in silence for a long while and tried to process it all. She'd heard all sorts of things about Byron Knight — what a tyrant he was, how cold he was, how he treated women — but being at the receiving end of his dismissal was humiliating and depressing, She was fighting tears when she stood up, gathered up the few things she had there in her office, and left.

For years, she'd worn a hard shell — an outer shell. Who cared what people thought of her? She simply chose not to care. She'd built up her defenses to keep people from getting inside her head or her heart, but somehow Byron had managed to do both.

No! She wouldn't even think such a thing. She was a successful woman, a woman who had a lot going for her and a busy road ahead of her. Why would she ever let a man mess with her head or make her think foolish schoolgirl thoughts? She wouldn't.

She barely remembered the drive from Knight Construction back to her accounting firm, but when she found herself parked in the garage beneath the building, she took a few moments to collect herself.

Zach would be thrilled to have her back, and even sooner than he'd been expecting. She fought down the tears that wanted to surface, looked in her small mirror, and gave herself a pep talk before she fell apart.

Only then did she struggle out of her car and grab her briefcase. It was time to get to work. She'd been trying to keep up, but doing two jobs made that impossible. She would forget all about Byron as soon as she sat down at her desk and turned on her computer.

Before she even had a chance to sit, Zach rushed headlong into her office. "Didn't we just get off the phone?" he said as she pulled out her chair.

"That we did," she replied with the best cheerful voice she could manage.

"Did something happen? Not that I'm complaining at having you here, but I wasn't expecting you. Are you okay? You look a bit…off." Zach's concern came through loud and clear.

Dammit! Tears welled up in her eyes, and there was now no way in hell that she'd be able to tell Zach there was nothing wrong. He sat there on the corner of her desk, silent for once, and he looked at her in shock. She understood that. She'd never so much as blinked before. It wasn't who she was. McKenzie took pride in the fact that she showed herself to the world only with the most perfect of poise.

Slowly, so slowly, as if approaching a snake, Zach slid down from her desk and actually knelt down in front of her. "You know you can talk to me, right? We're friends, McKenzie."

She wanted to laugh at that. She had no friends — well, maybe McKenzie could consider Jewell a friend now, but not really, if she thought about it. A friend knew you inside and out and loved you anyway. There wasn't a single living soul who knew the real her.

"I'm just an idiot, Zach, and I behaved like a typical

idiot does," she said, pushing back the tears with a will of iron forged on the anvil of a hard life.

"The last time I checked, doll, you were about the most brilliant person I've ever met, so we both know that's not true. Tell me about it. I swear it will make you feel better," he assured her.

She tried to hold back, but she felt her mouth open and the words pour out. "I had sex with Byron…a lot of sex," she muttered.

Her statement was met with silence. But then a smile appeared on Zach's face. "Well, he must be incredibly bad in the bedroom if you're looking so melancholy about it."

She was so flabbergasted by his words, she didn't know how to respond. It wasn't the reaction she'd been expecting, but then again, she had no clue what reaction to expect — she'd never had a conversation quite like this one before.

"Well…um…I…" How in the world did she respond to what Zach had just said?

"Did you enjoy yourself?"

Again, she was so stunned by his question, she actually answered him. "It was amazing." She was still in shock over that. Because of Nathan and that sicko rapist, she'd just assumed all sex was horrible. Never, ever could she have imagined how great it could actually be. If she were younger, *OMG* might come to mind.

"Well, then, I don't understand the tears. You're an adult, McKenzie and even though I'm a guy and I'm not supposed to say this, Byron Knight is one hot piece of ass. He's single; you're single. Enjoy the fact that you had some out-of-the-ballfield sex, and quit beating yourself up over it. It's okay to let down your hair once in a while," he told her, standing up and moving back to the door.

"I don't even know how to address anything you just said." She knew her mouth was hanging open as she spoke to him.

"You don't have to. Just close your eyes and picture that moment of ecstasy," he said with a sigh before his voice rose, startling her. "Damn, it's been too long since I've had sex!"

"Um…sorry," she told him, but finally she smiled.

"Since you're all warmed up, you could help me out…," he said with a lavish wink.

"I think I'll pass, if you don't mind," she told him, but she actually laughed.

"Sucks to be me. Okay, my sweet, I'm going to let you get some actual work done now," Zach told her. "If and when you need to vent again, call me in. I'm always here for you."

McKenzie thanked him and then sat back and looked around her office. It was where she'd been trying to get back to for the past three weeks and now it seemed so lonely, so devoid of life.

The first thing she was going to do this weekend was head out on a mission — some major shopping. It was time to add color to her life. She'd known when she went into this thing with Byron that it wasn't going to last, so she wouldn't let it keep her down.

No way, no how.

CHAPTER TWENTY-FOUR

I'M GLAD YOU decided to come."

McKenzie glanced up at Byron and her hard-won calmness instantly evaporated. She hadn't seen him since Monday morning, and she had gone back and forth on whether to show up at the fancy fundraiser.

She refused to give him a hint of the tremors that were rushing through her. "You promised me that it would be good exposure for my company for me to be here," she replied calmly.

"Yes, a lot of people are here tonight. You'll be able to make good contacts," he assured her as he offered her his arm.

They were at the legendary Anderson mansion, and she couldn't help but be happy to step inside its stately door. Yes, a number of jaw-dropping mansions could be found in this area, but none compared to the masterpiece Joseph Anderson had built for his wife over fifty years earlier.

The castle walls stood high, and the solid wooden doors opened to a home of marble and elegance unlike any other in the entire area. As she and Byron stepped inside, McKenzie had a difficult time holding in the gasp that she managed to suppress when first confronting the grand staircase and priceless works of art. And this was only the beginning.

She twisted a piece of her hair as she shifted from foot to foot. Yes, she'd run a high-class bordello, or whatever anyone wanted to call it, and, yes, she'd dealt with wealthy men for years, but she'd never, ever entered a home like this one.

"You are a stunning woman — a stunning *person* — and you fit in here, McKenzie. There's no need for you to be nervous," Byron whispered. "Remember that."

"How would you know if I'm nervous?"

"I can see it in your eyes and from the fidgeting you're doing. Hold your head up. You belong here."

She wanted to remind him of what he thought of her, but she was already feeling out of place, and she didn't need him to remember he though of her as nothing more than a two-cent whore. If he demeaned her, then her evening would be ruined. There was no way she wanted him aware that he had that sort of power of her, either.

Coming had been a mistake, but she'd been too tempted by the opportunity to draw in more business. And if she hadn't come with Byron, she never would have been invited to attend an event at the Anderson mansion. She was just grateful to be there, so she had little choice but to push down the nerves.

Placing his hand on her back, he led her forward to another huge room with six-foot-long crystal chandeliers dripping from the ceiling, music hanging in the air, and a polished waitstaff serving hundreds of guests.

"I can't imagine growing up in a home like this," McKenzie said. "How in the world did they ever keep track of their children?"

Byron laughed. "For one, I'm sure they have an army of staff members to take care of the home and keep an eye out for missing children. But any home that you make comfortable is a home. It doesn't matter if it's a one-bedroom apartment or a colossal mansion. When it comes down to it, they're are all the same," he said, and he accepted two glasses of champagne from a waiter.

McKenzie looked at him for a moment before speaking. "That's easy for you to say. This is obviously coming from a man who has never had to spend a day of his life in a small apartment."

"No, I haven't, but still…" He was wise enough to shut up on that subject before he changed topics altogether. "Do be careful while you're in this home. There are rumors that the family patriarch, Joseph Anderson, is quite the matchmaker. All three of his boys fell quickly into matrimony, and many who know the family say it had everything to do with their father. And then his nieces and nephews began marrying one by one," Byron said with another laugh.

McKenzie scoffed. "Say what? Their father —or the patriarch or whatever — can't make them get married."

"No. Joseph actually loves his sons, something you don't often see in wealthy families. Hell, the children are often raised by the nanny. But rumors say he helped… shall we say, prod them along."

"What do you mean by 'prod them along'?"

Byron glanced around. "He played matchmaker. He hired the perfect assistant for his oldest son, a cook for his youngest — that sort of thing," he said.

"Just because he hires certain people doesn't mean he's playing matchmaker," she pointed out.

He looked down at her with such intensity, she found herself barely able to hold on to her glass. "You know more than anyone what happens when too sexually compatible people begin working closely together," he said, taking her breath away.

"You're being inappropriate," she warned.

"Just filling you in on some local Anderson history. Not trying to be inappropriate at all," he said, but his hand caressed down the length of her partially covered back.

"Do I hear you speaking about me?"

McKenzie jumped at the loud voice right behind her, and then both of them turned, and she found herself looking up, up, up. She had thought Byron was tall — heck, he was six foot three — but the man with the white hair and a groomed white beard seemed a giant compared with Byron.

"Only in the most respectful of ways," Byron said. "How are you doing, Joseph?"

McKenzie was surprised to see genuine affection on Byron's face.

"I can't complain in my old age, Byron." His attention was quickly diverted to McKenzie, and he gave her an intense look. "And how are you, little missy?"

"I'm sorry, Joseph. I'm being rude," Byron said. "This is my date, McKenzie Beaumont"

McKenzie was flabbergasted. She didn't want to correct him in front of their host and tell the man she wasn't Byron's date, but at the same time, she also didn't want him thinking this was going to lead to a happy ending for anyone involved.

Joseph took the choice of her having to say anything at all away when his boisterous voice sounded again. "It's a pleasure to meet you, Ms. Beaumont. I hope you enjoy the party." He ignored her hand and gave her a half-hug.

"Um…it's a pleasure to meet you, too. Thank you for having me," she said. "And please call me McKenzie."

"McKenzie has recently opened up Seattle Accounting," Byron said, "and she supplies temporary or full-time staff if you ever need anyone."

"Is that so? I'll have to come in and see you on Monday," Joseph said. "Most certainly." Someone called out to him. "I'm sorry to rush off. You know how these parties go. But, I won't forget about Monday." And just like that, he was gone.

McKenzie could barely even think, let alone get words out at how excited she was at the prospect of having Joseph Anderson coming in to see her business. "Do you really think he'll come?" she asked. It was barely above a whisper.

"Joseph never says anything if he doesn't plan to follow through," Byron assured her.

"Oh, my gosh, Byron, do you have any idea what that would do for my company if he hired us?"

Byron laughed. "Hey. Am I now chopped liver?"

"Of course not!" she said as she grabbed his arm. "It's just that it's the Andersons…*The Andersons!*"

"Yeah, yeah, Seattle's royalty," he said, but with humor, not ill-will. Yes, the Andersons were a force to be reckoned with, but that didn't make him any less of a force, McKenzie thought.

"You're just pouting now," she told him, but her

nerves had completely evaporated. Her champagne had evaporated too, she realized, but before she could tell Byron she didn't need any more of it, another cup was placed in her hand, and she found herself sipping on it.

"Come on. We have more people to meet," hc said, taking her hand and squeezing it before he wrapped his arm around her. Then, she felt almost like royalty as they made their way across the beautiful marble floors and greeted a number of beautiful people in the process.

McKenzie got a rare glimpse into why Byron was such a successful man. Though he told everyone and anyone that he didn't particularly like his fellow human beings, he was a natural crowd-pleaser, a person who knew the exact words to say to both the men and women. She was in awe of his ability to shine.

"Ah, another important person for you to meet," Byron told her, and then she was standing in front of none other than Rafe Palazzo. He was standing next to a petite brunette wearing a gown that was worthy of the red carpet, and with emeralds so brilliant they seemed to outshine everything in the room.

"It's been a while, my friend," Rafe said, shaking Byron's hand.

"Yes, we both work far too much," Byron replied. "Rafe, this is my date, McKenzie Beaumont."

"What's a beautiful young woman doing with a man like this?" Rafe asked her, and he held out his hand.

Before McKenzie could answer, the woman next to him sent him a glare.

"Never mind my husband. He likes to shock people. I'm Ari."

"It's a pleasure to meet you both," McKenzie said. The

Palazzo family had come from Italy and then settled in San Francisco, where she had known of them. Everyone knew of them because they were beyond powerful. There was no way she could have grown up down there without knowing exactly who they were.

"Are you enjoying the party?" Rafe asked. "I have to say that Joseph sure knows how to throw one, and make sure the pockets of his guests are empty at the end of the night."

"Yes, that's for sure," Byron told him. "But he and his wife, Katherine, always pick the best charities, ones that deserve every dollar in donations, though, so I give without a second thought."

"That's very true," Rafe replied. "But the deductions don't hurt."

McKenzie stood there and listened, wondering whether she was too far out of her league. She wanted to hang out with people of this caliber, but at the same time she didn't even come close to their level. Was she trying too hard to carve out a name for herself? Were they all secretly laughing at her? She'd run an escort service, and now she was trying to run a respectable business. Was that just too much?

After she and Byron left Rafe and Ari, McKenzie was introduced to a number of other people, but the night became a blur of names and faces. How could she remember any of them when her mind was too focused on what Byron was doing with her and why he was telling everyone she was his date? And then there was the real question, the one she was afraid to ask.

What was going to happen when the two of them left the party?

CHAPTER TWENTY-FIVE

TRUST WASN'T AN easy thing for Byron to give. He gripped his glass and tried to pay attention to what the woman, whose name he'd already forgotten, was saying to him. But all he could do was watch as McKenzie leaned back and let out a peal of laughter.

It was a beautiful sound.

And the man making her laugh didn't realize his life was in jeopardy. Byron didn't do jealousy, but at the moment, the green-eyed monster had him in its grip, and his testosterone was spiking to dangerous levels.

No, he didn't think McKenzie was interested in leaving the fundraiser with another guy, but, again, trust didn't come easy for Byron.

His mother —more accurately, the woman who had given birth to him — had laughed like that, had flirted with men right in front of her husband. But there was a difference. His "mother" had gone to those men's beds, and she'd flaunted it in front of her husband, Byron's father.

She had been a stone-cold bitch — a whore to end all

whores — but all women were basically the same. Byron knew that. Sure, McKenzie was there with him tonight, but only because he had promised her she could meet all sorts of people who would come running in through her doors to buy her services.

Which services did she want to provide?

He downed the champagne in his glass, then took a step toward her. But he stopped himself. For the past few hours he'd been by her side. He could easily spend fifteen minutes without her.

And yet if that were so, why did everything inside of him want to walk up to her and stake his claim? *She* was bad for him, so very bad, and he couldn't seem to care that she was messing with his head.

He'd had an easy out. She was no longer working with him at Knight Construction. All he'd had to do was not call her, not ask her to this function, just go on with his life and forget he'd ever even heard about McKenzie Beaumont. But no. That's not what he'd done at all.

And now here they were. And he was furious with her and with himself. She hadn't done anything wrong this evening — in fact, she'd been the perfect companion, and his colleagues adored her. So he had no reason to feel this anger.

Maybe it was because he couldn't forget her taste or her scent. He couldn't get the sound of her voice from his head. Everything that she was lingered with him, refused to let go. He needed her, and he was a fool to think he didn't. He just wasn't sure how long he would need her for.

When she looked up and their eyes collided, her laughter stopped and the smile on her lips fell away. Ah, there it was. There was the passion he wanted to see. He refused to let her gaze go. He took another step forward, but someone passed in front of him, breaking the connection.

In that instant, McKenzie was no longer looking at him, but he saw the tension in her shoulders. She knew he was walking toward her, and he enjoyed that she was so aware of everything he did. He enjoyed everything about this woman. Even if he hated that he did.

When he finally reached her side, he slid his arm around her and he looked at the man she was chatting with. "I'm sorry I took so long," Byron said, his lips an inch from her ear, causing a shiver to run down her.

"I was just visiting with Lance Storm. He's one of Joseph's nephews. He's been entertaining me with some interesting work adventures," she said, her smile returning.

"That's nice," Byron said, not meaning it in the least. "I didn't know Joseph had any nephews with the last name Storm." Was this good-looking guy some sort of pathological liar?

"That's a very long story," Lance said. "We didn't actually know we were related to Joseph and George until a couple of years ago."

Byron snorted, and he asked, "How is that possible?"

"Our father was stolen at birth." Lance didn't even blink as he said it.

"Wait! I think I did hear something about this last year, but your family has done remarkably well at keeping the story from the papers," Byron said, the pieces coming together as he remembered how Joseph and his twin brother, George, had discovered they were actually from a set of triplets.

"My uncle Joseph is a great man, and people love and

respect him." Lance said. "Yes, whenever the Anderson family does something, it's newsworthy, but there's been very little said about my father coming into their lives. I don't expect that to last forever, unfortunately."

"Joseph did a pretty good preemptive strike with his press release, though," Byron replied. "He beat the tabloids to it. That's why the story temporarily fled my mind."

"Well, Byron, it's been a pleasure to speak with your beautiful date tonight, but I see my brother calling me, so I'm going to have to continue this conversation later."

He left, and Byron turned to McKenzie. He was more than ready for this party to end, to take her home, take her clothing off, and have her writhing beneath him. The night had dragged on long enough, and the last thing he wanted to see was her speaking with any more single men, or men who appeared single because they wore no wedding ring.

"Have you had a good evening?" he asked her in a tight voice as he began leading her toward the ballroom doors.

"Yes, it's been wonderful," she said. Then she realized where they were going. "Are we leaving so soon? It might be considered rude," she warned him.

"There are so many people here that no one will notice we've gone. I've already written my check," he said, still pushing her toward the exit.

Before they reached the doors, his brother Tyler stepped in front of them.

"Where are you two off to in such a hurry?" he asked, and he looked at them slyly.

"We've done the rounds," Byron practically growled. If they got interrupted one more time, he might do something stupid like throw her over his shoulder and make a serious dash out of there.

"You can't possibly be thinking of leaving, not when McKenzie looks so absolutely ravishing," Tyler said, turning his complete attention on McKenzie and making Byron's gut burn. Tyler leaned in and kissed her cheek before letting his eyes glance downward at the modest amount of cleavage she was showing.

Byron's gut clenched tighter as he thought seriously of smacking his little brother. He hadn't done in a lot of years.

"Thank you, Tyler," McKenzie said. That musical laugh came out again.

Tyler sent her a salacious grin, then turned his focus to Byron. "So… When did you two start hanging out outside the office?"

Byron sent a withering look to his brother.

"It's not a big deal," McKenzie said. "Byron just wanted to introduce me to his business associates. He's trying to help drum up more business for me."

Before Byron was able to contradict her, Tyler got a gleam in his eyes. Byron knew right then that he was going to have to stomp his little brother for sure before the night was finished.

"Well, McKenzie, if this isn't a date, then could I talk you into a dance?" Tyler asked.

"We're together," Byron said, the *R*s sounding fiercely when he spoke.

"Wait, I'm confused," Tyler replied, looking far too innocent. "I thought you were just here for business."

"Tyler, why don't you go find an eligible girl? McKenzie is off limits."

McKenzie stiffened beside him, but he didn't care. There was no way in hell he was going to watch his woman waltz off in his brother's arms. She was his and only his.

Tyler guffawed. "That was way too easy," he said. He patted Byron on the back, told McKenzie to have a great evening, and wandered off.

"What was easy?" McKenzie asked.

"My brother likes to play stupid little games," Byron told her, his temper settling down as he started to realize what an idiot he'd just been. "He's very good at them." Of course Tyler wasn't trying to make a move on McKenzie. The brothers liked to poke at each other, but they'd never do anything that crossed a certain line.

One of those lines was not to poach on the others' territory. Female territory. It had never been done, and it wouldn't be done.

"Okay, then…," she said, but she backed off and didn't complete her sentence.

He turned to her and looked into her eyes. He wanted no misinterpretation of what he was about to say. She sucked her breath in as he pulled her against him and brought his mouth to within an inch of hers.

"We are very much here on a date, McKenzie. We will leave here and go back to my place, and we will wake up in the morning very happy. Very laid-back. Very *laid*."

Her face heated and her breathing deepened, but she didn't say a word. He waited several heartbeats before he bent down and brushed his lips against hers. If she was going to tell him no, then it had better be now.

The flavor and savor of her lips exploded in his mouth, and Byron prayed to anything that would listen that she didn't suddenly decide she didn't want this. He was now, more than ever before, ready to leave and ready to take her to bed.

The desire he'd been living with from the moment

they'd first kissed was now a flow of molten rock through his veins. It had been almost a week since he'd had her, and his need to possess her was so overwhelming that he didn't know if he'd even make it back home.

"Tell me you're ready to leave, McKenzie."

She licked her lips, making him throb with need. He waited.

"Take me home," she finally whispered so quietly he barely managed to hear it. But hear it, he did.

He didn't waste any more time.

CHAPTER TWENTY-SIX

PLEASURE AND PAIN, pain and pleasure. They were all the same, and they were so very different. As Byron's lips glided down her throat, circled her peaked nipples, and trailed down her body to suck on the point where her throbbing was centered, McKenzie cried out.

The pleasure was to the point of pain — the agony and the ecstasy, to borrow a phrase. If she didn't come, didn't have release, she might actually vanish from existence. He made her body sing, and that was something no other man had done for her.

She had thought sex was solely for men, that there was no real pleasure in it for women, but in Byron's arms she found that wasn't true at all. Yes, he was a demanding lover, but he gave so much more than he took. She couldn't get enough of his touch, of his kisses, of the power of his lovemaking.

"Let's play, McKenzie."

"What?" she gasped, and she didn't even recognize the

sound of her own voice.

"I want to play. I want to put your body on display —
for me, and *only* for me — and do whatever I want with
you," he said, his lips winding their way back up her body.
"Do you trust me?"

Did she trust him? No. She knew he was going to break
her heart. But did she think he would hurt her? No. She
knew he wouldn't physically hurt her.

"Yes," she sighed as he sucked her nipple into his lips
and scraped it with his teeth. Her back arched in the air.

Then he was taking her hands, raising them above
her head, and suddenly she couldn't move them from
the binds. Panic filled her as she struggled to break free.
"What are you doing?"

Her eyes shot open and she looked into his passion-
filled gaze. "I'm taking you to a whole new realm of
pleasure," he assured her.

"No, not like this." She wrestled to break free.

"Give me one minute. If you still want your so-called
freedom in one minute, I will undo you. You can take the
reins. You can ride me to your heart's content. Hell, I won't
object — not for a minute."

Desire burned in his gaze, but something else, too,
something she had never seen before. If she were a fool,
she would have thought it was affection, but she knew that
couldn't possibly be. He desired her, but he didn't in any
way care about her.

She couldn't speak, so she nodded her head, and his
mouth descended, his lips ravishing hers as he ran his
hands up her sides and cupped her breasts, tweaking her
nipples with his eager fingers and making her cry out
again, making her forget all about the way he'd bound

her hands.

He moved down her stomach and then his mouth was on her core, his tongue moving rhythmically against her quivering flesh, her arousal growing, nearing explosion.

Somehow he knew each time she came closer and closer to release, and he backed off, moving his tongue down her soft folds and then slowly drawing it up again to the point she wanted his touch most.

"Please, please…" she cried out, but she couldn't grab his head, couldn't keep him where she so desperately wanted him.

"Not too fast, McKenzie," he growled, his words vibrating against her thigh.

He let his mouth move back up her body, and then he was on his knees, rising above her, his beautiful satin manhood so close to her face. "Taste me," he commanded her, and he rubbed his arousal against her mouth.

She opened her lips greedily, and she circled her tongue around the head of his desire, tasting the muskiness and wanting more. He gave her only an inch, then two, but he refused to give her what she wanted. "I'm the one who controls this," he said, his words strained.

"You want my mouth around you. Admit it, Byron."

He stroked her breasts while she sucked on him as far as he allowed. Then he pulled away, only to drop down her body and suddenly he was pushing two fingers inside her. He began driving them in and out at the same speed as he thrust his arousal in her mouth.

But she wanted more. She wanted him buried inside her with his mouth on hers. She wanted release. She wanted to make love — yes, *love* — then make love again. This moment could last an eternity and it still wouldn't be long enough.

Without warning, her body exploded, her core grabbing his fingers and holding them inside her as wave after wave of pleasure washed through her. He pulled his arousal from her mouth and his fingers from her heat, and then she was alone.

She nearly fell asleep when she heard a sound, and instantly her body reawakened. She wanted more. And she knew she was going to get it.

Byron untied her hands, then rubbed her arms from wrist to shoulder and back again. All the while, his body lay next to hers, his manhood pushing up against her leg, making her squirm beside him.

Then he rose up and pulled her from the bed, so both of them were standing beside it. "You are so unbelievably sexy, McKenzie. I could almost come from nothing more than looking at you," he said as he moved his hands down her naked torso, making her knees nearly collapse.

"I hope you plan on doing more than looking, Byron. I'm not finished," she said, a throaty groan escaping as he tweaked her nipples with seductive fingers.

"I'll never be finished with you," he said, and she almost wished that were true. She could do this forever.

He turned her around, and she nearly protested, but he encircled her with his hands and rubbed the underside of her breasts. And as he held their weight in his palms, her nipples peaked painfully hard.

One of his hands drifted up past her throat and settled on the back of her neck, while the other dipped to her stomach and held her tightly against him, letting her feel his thickness on the crease of her shapely ass.

He pushed against her back, and she leaned forward,

arching her derrière into the air, his solid erection resting against it. Then he moved back, sliding his arousal downward along her swollen folds and wet the head with her juices.

McKenzie wriggled against him, wanting him inside her, ready to feel more of the pleasure only he could give her.

"Patience," he whispered as he bent down and ran his tongue along her spine. He dropped to his knees and kissed his way along her backside and down to her thighs before pushing her legs apart and coating his tongue with her heat.

When she was just about to release again, he stood, and before she could take a single breath, he was back behind her, gripping her hips and then thrusting forward, forcefully pulling out and pushing back in.

She exploded around him, her legs shaking, her body clenching his thick arousal as she nearly wept with the pleasure of his movements. He was inside her up to the hilt in this position, and she was greedy for every single inch of him. Those inches certainly added up.

When her pulsations finally stopped, he slowed his thrusts. For a brief moment she felt again both the pain and the pleasure of overstimulation. She wanted to push him out — it was too much. But he let his hands glide back around her body, and while one found a breast, the other touched the sensitive bundle of nerves right above where his hardness was penetrating her.

And she felt her pleasure build once more. Greed. This was what greed felt like, because she wanted it all. She wanted him over and over again.

With desperation born of that greed, she began pushing

back against him to meet his thrusts. The sound of their bodies slapping together served only to heighten her pleasure. He groaned loudly, and she reached back to find his tightened balls, and she squeezed gently. He let out a cry and then began shaking as he pumped hard inside her.

With a cry of her own, McKenzie shattered again, their sounds of pleasure blending together as they collapsed forward onto the bed. Byron lay on her back, and neither of them breathed evenly.

After several moments, he shifted off her, then climbed up onto the bed, pulling her with him, locking his arms around her.

"We're good together," he said, his hand in her hair, their bodies sated — for at least the next few minutes.

McKenzie said nothing. She was too afraid that this moment would end. Yes, they were good together.

But for how long?

CHAPTER TWENTY-SEVEN

AN ENTIRE WEEK passed with no word from Byron. Great sex — then nothing.

McKenzie knew this was how it was going to end, but even knowing that didn't help. Why should she be so upset? It wasn't as if she hadn't been through worse…a lot worse. She had been through hell and back a few times, and that a guy had used her for sex — great sex, mind you — and had then thrown her away shouldn't make her feel as if she didn't know which way was up anymore.

But each time she got a text message or the phone rang, her heart skipped a beat. What did it even matter? If he called or asked to see her, she would respond with an emphatic no. They were done. She wouldn't be used by him. By anyone.

Sitting at her desk back at Seattle Accounting, trying to do her job, she listened to her phone ring and took several deep breaths before answering it. She didn't care if it was Byron on the other end of the line, although she knew it wasn't. And no, it wasn't.

But no matter how many times she told herself this, she couldn't get past the little ache in her chest each time it wasn't him. Someday this would stop. Until then, she needed to just go on living her life.

She couldn't take any more today. There was just no way. Deciding to call it an early day, she let Zach know she was leaving, gathered her purse and coat, and left the building.

It was a typical cool autumn day in Seattle — if any days or any weather could be called typical anymore — and the last thing she wanted to do at three in the afternoon was return to her empty house. She had loved that home from the moment she'd walked through its doors knowing it was hers. But now it was just another place where she was all alone.

When had being alone been a burden? She'd survived a long time on her own, and she really shouldn't care, but after being with Byron — no matter how short a time it had all lasted — she was discovering she didn't want to be alone anymore.

She walked down the street two blocks over to her favorite pub, or what she hoped could still be her favorite pub, now that it was tainted with memories of being there with Byron, and stepped through the doors. The familiar noise, smell, and feel of the place helped soothe her nerves.

She moved to the back, sat down, and soon placed her order. Routine. That's what she needed. The more uniform her life was, the more she would appreciate it. Soon, she wouldn't have to think about Byron at all. Her life would just go back to the way it had always been.

"I hope you don't mind some company, sweet cheeks."

McKenzie looked up with disgust as Nathan plopped

down across from her.

"I do, actually. What in the hell are you doing here?"

"Awww, don't be like that, love. I just wanted to visit," he said, his weasel-like smirk in place.

"A smarter man would take a hint and stay the hell away when it's obvious he's not wanted around," she said to goad him.

His eyes narrowed, but then he leaned back and smiled. The waitress came up and he ordered a drink before McKenzie could tell the woman he wouldn't be staying long.

"I've missed you, McKenzie," he said, reaching across the table and grabbing her hand before she could yank it away.

"I don't know why you've decided to appear in my life again, Nathan. But you were the worst mistake I've ever made, and that's saying a lot," she said, "since I've made a lot of mistakes. I don't want to be anywhere near you. I don't want you around. If you can't take a hint and disappear, then I guess the law will help you to." She tugged against his hold, but she was reluctant to cause a scene in the bar, and he had to be well aware of that.

"I screwed up when you were younger. We all make mistakes. I think we could be good together, though, now that we're both older and wiser," he told her.

Bile rose in her throat when he caressed the top of her hand with his thumb.

"Are you listening to yourself? You drugged me and let a man rape me. That's not screwing up. That's assault," she said. What a worthless excuse for a human being. She was flabbergasted.

"Look, I'm nearly broke, and I have nothing and

nowhere to go. You've done well for yourself..." He shrugged, finally releasing her hand.

"Yes, I have done well, in spite of the way you treated me, of what you did to me, and what you planned on doing to me. I feel nothing but disgust for you — isn't that obvious? — and I don't ever want to have anything to do with you again. Leave me alone, leave this city if you have any sense, and stay the hell away from me," she snapped.

"You are such a hypocritical bitch. Yeah, I may have drugged you for that first time, but you sure snatched up the money quick and spent it on who knows what, and then you opened up your own little whorehouse where you did the exact same thing that I did," he said, his voice quiet but fierce.

"I did take the money, and I did run, to get as far away from you as possible. And I opened up that place to stop men like you from taking advantage of innocent women. The women I hired? I saved them; I helped them to have a better life. I don't care what you do with your life, Nathan. I don't care if you rot in the streets. You will never again take advantage of me, and you won't threaten or blackmail me. Our time is done. If I see you again after today, I will simply call the cops. As you damn well know, I've done it before."

She looked him in the eyes, knew she couldn't back down. Men like Nathan needed a weak woman to survive; they needed easy prey to feast upon. She was no longer vulnerable, no longer weak. And now that he'd lost his power over her, he would cower before her and run away with his tail tucked between his legs.

And just as she'd expected, he slumped a little, defeat on his face. "You owe me," he muttered.

"I owe you nothing," she snarled. "Now get the hell away from me."

She felt nothing but contempt for this man. When he didn't move immediately, she pulled out her phone. After that little incident at her house, she had a restraining order out on the man. And he knew it.

She started dialing the police and he immediately stood up. "Fine, I'm going," he said, his voice almost a wail.

"And don't come back."

He just nodded and walked away.

McKenzie leaned back after he left. Her life was far from perfect, but she knew this was the last time she would see that man. He was weak and pathetic, and the second she'd shown him some real backbone, it was obvious that the scumbag would go away.

If only she could show so much backbone with Byron. If only she could tell him she wanted to be with him. That just wasn't going to happen. It was over between them, and the sooner she accepted that, the quicker she would be able to heal.

CHAPTER TWENTY-EIGHT

BYRON WATCHED MCKENZIE leave her place of business, and before he could call out to her, she was around the corner. He followed, planning to talk to her. But before he was able to do so, she stepped into the small put he'd ate at with her and Jewell and sat down. He followed close behind, but his plans were thwarted when he ran into Tyler.

"What in the world are you doing here?" his brother said. "This is so not your kind of place."

"I'm meeting someone," Byron replied, watching McKenzie seat herself at the same table he'd joined her and his sister-in-law at.

"Well, have a drink with your little brother first. I haven't seen you in a couple of weeks," Tyler said.

"I don't have time right now."

"You don't have time for your brother?" Tyler raised an eyebrow.

"Let's meet tomorrow," Byron told him, still staring over at McKenzie's table. That's when he watched a man approach and sit down. Fury flooded over him. It wasn't as if he hadn't known she was a slut, but to see it firsthand made his stomach turn. "On second thought, I have time for a drink," he said, and he took a bar stool next to Tyler. But he kept staring over at McKenzie's table.

"What in the hell are you looking at so intently?" Tyler asked.

Before his brother could focus in on McKenzie, Byron distracted him. "I heard you're seeing a new woman," he said, and Tyler whipped his head around.

"Where did you hear that?" his brother asked.

"I have my sources," Byron said. Then fury overmastered him all over again when the man sitting with McKenzie took her hand.

He wanted to go over there and stake his claim, tell this man, whoever he was, that McKenzie was his, and that he'd better keep his filthy hands off her if he knew what was good for him. But he turned away and focused on his brother instead.

It was better for him that he'd seen this, better for him to accept what she really was. He'd forced himself not to talk to her all last week, tried to tell himself he didn't need or want her. But then, against his will, he'd found himself approaching her office building. He wanted her. It was as simple as that. If wanting anything, especially a woman, could be called simple.

"Did Blake say something to you?" Tyler asked him.

That caught Byron's attention.

"What? So you can confide in Blake but not in me?" Byron was surprisingly hurt by this revelation.

"No, Byron, it's not that. It's just that Blake and I have talked some. He's…I don't know, he's just so in love. Don't you ever want that?" Tyler asked.

Byron's gaze turned involuntarily back to McKenzie, who was still holding hands with the mystery man, and his heart flared. "No." He said the word curtly at best.

"I think you're lying," Tyler told him. "I think you want it, but you're afraid." He sounded so sad.

"Don't feel sorry for me," Byron growled. "I can have anything I want. And if it were love I wanted, I would have it. In a heartbeat."

"I don't think so, brother. I think you're afraid. Afraid because of what our mother was. But not all women are her."

Before Byron could reply, someone approached. "I'm sorry I'm so late," she said, stepping close to Tyler, a clear sign of possession.

"It's not a problem," Tyler replied. "I was talking to my brother here."

"Oh, your brother!" she exclaimed, and she turned shockingly bright blue eyes toward Byron. "I'm Elena. It's a pleasure to meet you." Before he could stop her, she leaned in and gave him a hug.

"What ever happened to handshakes?" Byron commented, and he watched a flare of hurt enter her eyes before she smiled through it.

"Sorry. I'm impulsive," Elena told him.

"We'll leave you to brood, big brother," Tyler said. He stood up and put his arm around Elena, and they walked away.

So Byron had ticked off his little brother. That was nothing new.

He almost missed it, but the man who was sitting with McKenzie pushed back his chair, and that's when he noticed the stress on her face. What in the world was going on? Was the man breaking up with her? Okay, she was going from one guy to the next, but Byron wasn't satisfied to leave it at that. Things were over with him and McKenzie, but he still needed answers. As he watched the man walk out of the pub, he decided to follow him.

The guy didn't make it far. About a block down the street he entered another bar and sat down. He ordered a cheap beer, piquing Byron's curiosity even more. Byron sat down next to him and ordered a whiskey, noticing the guy looking at it like it was gold.

"Hey there," Byron said in greeting as he downed his shot, and the man he'd targeted practically drooled over the drink.

"Hey," he grumbled as he sipped on his cheap beer. The man didn't look so good. What was McKenzie doing with a guy like him? He obviously had no money, so what good would the guy be to her?

"Looks like you've had one hell of a day. Let me get you a whiskey," Byron said as he ordered another one for himself and one for the piece of crap next to him.

"Sounds great," the man said, instantly perking up as the bartender set the glasses in front of them. Byron decided he needed to stay sober for this conversation, and he wanted the man drunk.

So he ordered a few more rounds, quickly dumping his own in the potted plant sitting conveniently there next to him at the end of the bar. The guy didn't even notice, he was so focused on his own drinking. And after about fifteen minutes, the man was thinking that Byron was his new best friend.

"My name's Nathan," he slurred.

"Great to meet you, Nathan. What has you in here before five?" Byron asked, as he held his hand up to order another round.

"Women!" the man grumbled.

"I hear you there. None of them can be trusted," Byron said, to spur him on. The sad thing was that he felt this way. He couldn't trust women.

Nathan's eyes lit up as he found himself in the company of another woman-hater. Byron had to know what McKenzie was doing with this guy. It was making less and less sense.

"Seriously! You try to help out one of those bitches and they turn on you and stab you in the back," the man spluttered, getting more and more worked up as he spoke.

Byron got him another drink.

"I've been there, man. I would love to put them in their place," Byron said, but he felt sick even saying the words out loud. No, he didn't respect women, but that didn't mean he felt they should be abused. He had Bill to thank for setting him straight on that.

"Yeah, I was just with my bitch of an ex tonight. I helped her out a lot. I gave her the know-how to start a successful career, and how does she thank me? By telling me to get lost, and getting a damn restraining order placed on me," Nathan grumbled.

This wasn't what Byron was expecting at all. "Sounds like a typical woman to me," is what he said.

"Yeah, typical. Screw that whore!"

"How did you help her?" Byron casually asked.

"I found her when she was young, real young, and innocent, you know?" Nathan said with demented glee in his eyes.

Byron instantly tensed. He suspected he wasn't going to like what came out of this man's mouth. "Tell me," he said, and the man was too wasted to notice Byron was no longer quite as friendly as before.

"Yeah, she was just eighteen, all roses and kittens, though her little sister was in some sort of coma or something and it was messing with her head. All I had to do was play the role of her prince come to save her. She was eating out of my hands within a few weeks," he said with a disgusting smile as he remembered back.

"Well, that doesn't sound like anything new. All women will eat out of your hand if you rescue them," Byron said, scoffing, as if the man was boring him.

That did the trick. Nathan obviously wanted to feel important, wanted Byron to see how much power he had. He was too drunk to realize that what he said next could land him in jail — if not dead when Byron's fists connected with his face.

"So I worked for a man who had a special client list. His clients liked innocent young things. They paid a lot of money for them."

"Sounds normal," Byron said, though his stomach was turning.

"Well, my ex ruined my life! She deserved everything she had coming. She was evil, though she hid it behind an innocent face. She was also so damn stupid. It's okay, though, because I showed her for the true whore she was, and the bitch had no idea what was coming for her. She wanted me, so why not give it up to someone else first for a lot of money? I knew I could have her over and over after that. I don't mind sharing my cows, if you know what I mean."

"Yeah, I know what you mean," Byron said, not sure if he could listen to any more of this.

"Well, the bitch got what she wanted, and then acted horrified when it was done, like she didn't secretly want it. I know she did. She was sure hot to trot, and she snapped up the money and then went running so fast I didn't have a shot at catching her."

"So how did you find her again?" Byron asked through clenched teeth as he motioned for the bartender to give the man another drink. He didn't want any chance that he'd sober up now.

"She opened a whorehouse," Nathan said. "I taught her how to do the tricks and then she opens a whorehouse and uses what I taught her to give herself a nice little life. Then the whore acts offended when I come back, acts like she didn't want it. She don't care that I have nothing. All she cares about is herself." His shoulders sagged as he leaned against the bar, too drunk now to even hold himself up.

"That sounds tragic," Byron said. He realized he wasn't going to get anything else out of this man. What he really wanted to do was put his hands around Nathan's throat and squeeze until the guy's eyes bulged from his bloated head.

"Yeah, I didn't even have a chance to taste her goodies, if you know what I mean, and even now they are some fine goodies. Dammit! I made her, so I should at least get to try a piece."

Byron was done with the conversation. His head was spinning with what this man had said. Should he believe the story? Byron just wasn't sure. That look of disgust and relief on McKenzie's face as Nathan had walked away from her at the bistro was burned into Byron's mind though.

She hadn't wanted this guy. But was it because he brought back her past? Or was it because he had hurt her feelings? He just didn't know what to believe anymore.

Without another word, he paid his tab and walked away from the bar. He needed to talk to someone he did trust, and the list of those people was incredibly short.

CHAPTER TWENTY-NINE

BYRON JUMPED INTO his car and headed immediately toward Bill's house. He needed to have some of these cobwebs cleared from his brain. He was more confused than ever before, and there was only one person he actually trusted on this earth who had known his parents and his grandparents.

As he pulled up to the house, Byron couldn't help but smile. It was a modest place, and he'd spent many long and lazy afternoons there as a child. When McKenzie had told him he didn't know what it was like to be in a small place, he could have corrected her, but he'd chosen not to. There had been no reason for her to know that for a few years at least, he'd had a somewhat normal childhood in a modest home. A home that had been filled with love.

Bill had made the boys do chores, teaching them how to have a good work ethic. If truth were to be told, he enjoyed working up a sweat. It was good for the body and the mind. That's something Bill had taught him when he was young.

It didn't take Bill long to answer the door and invite
Byron in. "Wow, two visits in such a short period, and
you're still wearing the same expression I saw on your
face last time. What in the world is going on in your life,
my boy?"

"I just…I need to talk to you."

"Well, let me get some food and drink. This looks like
it could take some time," Bill told him. Before Byron could
say anything, Bill was sitting him down at the kitchen table
while he went and rummaged through the fridge.

"I want to know why my dad did it. I want to know
why he stayed with my mother when she was destroying
his life."

Bill paused briefly and the refrigerator door stood
open. He finally finished pulling out the pitcher of what
Byron assumed was iced tea, then he set it on the table and
grabbed two glasses and a bag of chips and some artichoke
dip.

He sat down and looked at Byron for several long
seconds before he spoke. "Are you sure you should keep
bringing up the past and dwelling on it? I would think it's
time you started looking forward instead of backward,"
he finally said before pouring their tea and leaning back.
"I've been told that it's no damn good to drive when you're
staring in the rearview mirror."

"I need to know why he did it. Did my mother hold
something over him? Why else would he stay with her
when she was so awful, and when she despised him?"

"Even though your mother truly was a cold hearted
bitch. She turned into that. It wasn't something she started
as. I think life shapes you into the person you become, but
it is still a choice how you choose to treat others," Bill said

with a sigh. "Your father certainly wasn't a saint, either, Byron. It's something I haven't wanted to tell you, but he made several wrong turns himself. But is that important? I don't see how any of this can help you."

"My father was beaten down, and she was the one who did it," Byron replied. "Of course he wasn't a saint. He allowed it."

"He's the one who started it," Bill said with a long sigh.

"Wait! What are you talking about? Start from the beginning, dammit."

"Don't use that tone on me, young man," Bill warned him.

"I'm sorry, Bill. But please, just tell me the truth."

"Your mom and dad met when they were young. She had high aspirations in life, wanting to have a career, a family, and a lot of money. But then your father walked in the door. The man you knew was nothing like the young man he used to be. He was full of life, full of confidence — a lot like Tyler, actually. He was good-looking and he knew it, but he was the life of the party with no chips on his shoulder like the ones you and Blake have worn for so long."

"That's not fair. I have reasons for having those chips," Byron said in self-defense.

"I'm not saying you don't. I'm just saying that your father was a cocky, fun-loving son of a bitch at one time, and he enjoyed the ladies, lots and lots of ladies." Bill snorted in disgust.

Byron prodded him. "But then he met my mother..."

"He met her at a party," Bill said. "She was there with some friends, a chance meeting, but your father was immediately attracted to her. When he wasn't able to...

um…bed her that first night, his fascination grew. He chased her. She knew about your father and his reputation. Girls talk too, and she wanted nothing to do with him. That made your father chase her all the harder."

"I honestly can't picture my father as a 'lady-killer.' He was just such a weak guy when I was a child."

"You reap what you sow, boy." Bill took a drink before continuing. "It took him months, and by the time your mother agreed to go out with him, he was completely infatuated with her.

"They dated for a few months, and she eventually fell head over heels in love. You see, at one time she actually did believe in love and romance and what a lot of people call happily-ever-afters. That ended about a year into their marriage," Bill said with a sad shake of his head.

"Why?"

"Because as soon as your father had her toeing the line, he went back to his wild ways. Of course, he kept it hidden from her until after the wedding. He needed to have a beautiful wife to produce beautiful children, but he didn't want to give up his extracurricular activities. Almost as soon as they returned from the honeymoon, she found him with her best friend in her own bed."

"Ouch. That had to hurt." Though Byron used those words, he felt zero sympathy for what his mother might have been feeling.

"Yeah, it did. And your dad didn't even promise to never do it again. He said she could shut up and give him the kids he wanted, and in turn, he would give her the lifestyle she wanted. She was already pregnant with Blake, and she knew to leave him would mean a life of poverty and hardships trying to raise the child. You see, your father assured her he'd disown the kid and leave her with nothing. She'd signed an airtight prenup," Bill said.

"How do you know all of this?" Byron asked.

"I've been around a long time, Byron," Bill told him.

"Go on."

"After she had Blake, she changed. Her strength — if you want to call it that — increased, and she gave back to your father what he'd been giving to her. She slept with every guy she could find, and she grew colder and colder. She pulled away from you and Blake. And…" Bill stopped himself.

"What?" Byron demanded.

"There's more to it with Tyler, but I won't share his secrets," Bill said with another sad shake of his head.

"I need to know!"

Bill ignored that, but he continued with his story. "Your father had a minor stroke. Maybe drugs, maybe fate — I don't know — but it changed him. He was no longer such a devil-may-care guy. He'd met his own mortality and he begged your mother to forgive him. It was her turn to tell him to shut up and do what he was told. That's the man you knew, the man who appeared to be so beaten down."

"Whipped," Byron said.

"In a way he was, but they equally killed their love for each other. Now I'm not saying what your mother did in the end was acceptable. Far from it. I'm just saying that when two people set out to destroy each other, there's going to be a very unhappy ending."

Byron sat back in stunned silence. This sort of thing didn't happen in real life, did it? Not really. How could these two people who had given him life be so monstrous? How could he ever trust love? Hell, how could he ever trust himself? He didn't think he could.

"I know what you're thinking, and you're wrong," Bill insisted. "Just because your parents made mistakes doesn't mean that everyone is evil — women or men. If you have a chance at love, grab it and don't make the mistakes your parents made."

"It doesn't sound like anyone really knows what love is," Byron said slowly. "Unless you count Foreigner."

"I loved my wife completely, from the first day I met her until the day she died. No. That's not even true. I still love her now and it's been a few years since I've gotten to hold Vivian in my arms. She was my everything. And because I had her, my life was a much better place to be."

"You're certainly the exception to the rule, then, Bill, because you're the only person I know who had a good marriage."

"Your brother has a very good marriage, and soon he'll have a baby," Bill pointed out.

"Maybe it just looks good on the outside."

"And maybe you should have a little more faith. Have you ever seen Blake look happier?"

"No, but what guarantee do you have that it will last forever?"

"And so we've finally come to why you're really here," Bill said with a smile. "And I hate to tell you this, but there are no guarantees in life, Byron. I couldn't have said without a doubt that my beautiful wife would love me forever, but she chose to do just that, just as I chose to cherish her and love her beyond the grave. When you marry someone — hell, when you just love someone — you're taking a leap of faith. You are giving something of yourself, and to truly love someone, you can't expect anything back from them, not even their love."

"That makes no sense," Byron said. He stood up from the table and walked to the window, dragging his hands through his hair. "I need it to make sense. I need it to be black and white."

"Love isn't black and white," Bill told him. "It's multicolored, and multidirectional, and it will take you on the best ride of your life. But you can't even begin the adventure until you give your heart away."

Bill became silent, and, with his heart aching, Byron looked out the window at the empty field behind his mentor's house. There was so much information passing through his brain he didn't know what to do with it.

"You're in love with McKenzie, aren't you?" Bill asked.

Byron shook his head. No. He wouldn't and couldn't say that, but he felt a strange sensation in his throat and knew right then that he was in denial. Somehow, against his will, he had fallen for this woman, he had given her a piece of himself. He'd given her a piece of his heart. And what really frightened him was that he didn't know if he wanted to get it back.

He'd sat there with her scum of an ex and heard what the man had said, and he knew Nathan was a liar. He knew the man had probably put her through hell, and then some, and he knew there was no way McKenzie could ever be the monster he'd wanted her to be. She was strong and kind, and she had been through a lot. He didn't want to hurt her anymore.

"I need to go," Byron said, overwhelmed with what he had heard and the way he was feeling.

"I understand that, but if you take anything with you today, Byron, then take this. If you can't let go of the demons of your past, and you care anything at all for this woman, you have to let her go. Don't punish her for mistakes she hasn't made. She's not your mother, and you aren't your father. You're better than that. To love someone is to truly want the best for them — even if that's letting them go."

"I don't know what I'm going to do," Byron had to say.

"You'll make the right choice," Bill told him. "It's just who you are."

As Byron drove away from Bill's house, he realized that the man who had stepped in and raised him and his brothers had a lot more faith in him than he had in himself. But he didn't know if he could be that man that Bill saw. Not even for McKenzie.

CHAPTER THIRTY

WHAT ARE YOU doing here?"

That was the question of the hour, Byron thought. He'd gone straight from Bill's to McKenzie's front door, and now that he was standing there, he hadn't the foggiest idea what to say to her.

"Byron?" Her blank expression changed to one of concern, and it was that look on her face that snapped him out of his trance.

"I wanted to talk," he said. "Can I come in?"

She looked at him suspiciously for a few tense moments before speaking again. "I don't think we have anything else to talk about, Byron."

"I met Nathan tonight."

Those four short words zapped all the color from her face, and she stared at him in shock. What he wouldn't pay to know what was going through her mind right now.

"I don't understand…" Her voice had grown hoarse.

"I saw you with him at the restaurant we went to with Jewell a few weeks ago. I followed him," Byron told her.

"Why would you do that?" she asked, gripping the sweater she was wearing.

"I was jealous," he admitted.

"Why in the world would you be jealous? You…you…" She was so stunned, she lost her ability to form words.

"Please just tell me what happened when you first met him." Byron was practically begging.

She opened the door wider, allowing him in. He didn't question her; he just followed her into the living room, where she walked over to a window and stared out into the darkness.

"I told you about the crash, the one that put my sister in a coma when she was only fourteen. And you know that my mother blamed me for it. . ." When she paused, Byron made sure not to move a muscle for fear that she would clam back up. But she soon started speaking again.

"After four years of my mother's bitter rages, drinking, and constant blame, I'd had enough. I felt guilty about being angry at her, at my sister, at the world, but I had to get away. I got a job at a small café, rented a room near the local college, and thought I was doing pretty dang well for myself. I would go visit my sister occasionally, but every time I did, my anger would build back up. My life had been hell since the wreck, and there were so many times I wished I were the one in that bed, the one oblivious to it all. But those thoughts gave me even more reason to feel guilty, because at least I had a life to live, while she didn't. No matter what I did, I was always racked with guilt back then…"

"You were just a kid, McKenzie."

"Don't, Byron. I've heard that a million times. If you don't let me talk, then I'm not going to be able to get through this."

"I'm sorry. Please go on." He wanted to reach for her, but he knew she was fragile and he wanted her to continue.

"When I turned nineteen, met what I thought was a sophisticated, beautiful man. He was ten years older than me, but that was all part of the appeal. He had this smile that seemed to light up an entire room, and he came into the diner for months, flirting with me, and only with me, even though there were far prettier waitresses working there."

"I find that hard to believe," Byron mumbled before shutting up again.

"Even though I was so young, I'd been living with trauma all through my teenage years. Impressionable years, or so they call them. I never dated — hell, I'd never even kissed a guy at that point. I was shy and didn't know what to think about all of the attention I was getting from this man. So when he asked me out on a date, I just nodded yes. I couldn't even get words to come from my mouth."

Byron felt thwarted when McKenzie closed her eyes briefly. When her eyes were open, he could read her expressions like a book, and he didn't want to be shut out right now.

She continued before he had to prompt her. "We went on several dates over the next two months, and I fell irrevocably in love with the man. Well, *irrevocably* isn't quite the word, but that's the way it seemed. He always walked me to my door, kissed me goodnight, and never tried to push it further than that. We would talk about sex, and at first, I was terrified to even consider it, but then the kisses grew a little longer, and I began feeling things inside me I never thought I would feel — sensations I thought only existed in romance novels. So I told him I wanted to try...you know...soon." The words seemed to burn her as she spoke them.

"One night he took me to his house, or what I thought was his house. It was on the outskirts of town, big, expensive — the kind of place where real artwork hung on the walls, not just prints," she said with a bitter laugh.

"McKenzie..." Byron was beginning to feel bad about forcing her to take this stroll down the ugliest possible memory lane.

She continued anyway and he didn't stop her. "We sat down and he poured some wine, very good wine..." Another pause. And this time there were tears in her eyes again when she looked at him. "And then everything went black. When I woke up, I was in a big, horrible bed, lying...naked beside a man I didn't know. My entire body hurt, and I was bruised all over. I was terrified. I slipped from his bed, found my clothes on the floor, threw them on, then quickly ran from the house. Nathan was waiting outside in his car.

"I thought we were dating, but it turns out that he was really just a pimp, a guy who made a lot of money at his job. He found inexperienced young women — of course, they had to be virgins — and he wined and dined them, made sure they were a perfect fit, a girl without ties, a girl who no one would ever believe if she cried 'rape,' and then he matched them with a john who would pay a lot of money for a night of...'pleasure.'"

"Crap, McKenzie..." He should stop this, but he didn't.

"The man I'd been dating wasn't really dating me," she said. "He was prepping me to be his next call-girl. When it was the first time for a virgin woman, he always got paid a lot of money, and then, after that first time, some of the girls stayed on with him. He paid them more than they'd make in their pathetic restaurant jobs, and his clients were…how do I put this?" She took a deep breath. "Men with a certain tastes, but men who could pay a lot for their twisted lifestyles."

"Like the men you catered to at Relinquish Control," Byron said. What the hell? Why would she have opened a place that provided services like that if she'd been through such a traumatizing experience? As if she could read his mind, she addressed that next.

"I took the blood money I had earned from him and I ran far away. It took me a couple of years, but I saved every dime, made a few very good investments, and then I got the idea for Relinquish Control. Not to take power away from women, but to give it back to them. My girls had nothing, and I saved them from the streets. I took the control away from the men who make women's lives hell. Those men had to come to me, and they had to sign a contract, and my girls' safety was ensured. I had pictures of the men, their ID, everything to identify them if one of my girls disappeared. The man who raped me got away with it. Nathan Guilder got away with it. I wasn't letting other men get away with anything."

"You can't stop it from happening," Byron told her.

"No. You're right. I can't stop it, but I saved a lot of girls. My escorts weren't naïve, inexperienced little things. They were experienced and they chose to better their lives. None of them stayed more than two years. They saved their money, then moved on. Exactly like I did," she said, lifting her chin, challenging him to call her a whore again.

"I…I…" Byron was at a complete loss for words.

"It's fine, Byron. I get it. You assume that I'm a whore, that if I make my living a certain way, it's because I'm insatiable. And to add to that, I didn't make it exactly hard for you to get me into your bed," she said, a humorless laugh escaping her lips.

"You were fourteen when you basically lost your sister, your mother and your father. I'm sorry if I've been harsh on you," Byron told her.

He didn't know what to think. He knew in his gut that she was telling the truth. But just because she'd been through hell didn't mean that she was innocent. It just meant that she was a real person. That was something he could no longer ignore.

"I needed to make a lot of money. My sister's care wasn't cheap," she said, laughing humorlessly again.

"Why didn't you just let her go? By the time you opened the doors to Relinquish, she'd been in a coma for about ten years."

She looked at him like he was a monster before replying. "You never give up on the people you love," she told him sternly.

"No, but you can also forgive yourself for mistakes you made as a kid, and for making a mistake with this Nathan guy."

"That's really easy for you to say, Byron. You were born into wealth and privilege. Life hasn't continually kicked you back down every time you tried to stand up again. In this world, you're either a winner or a loser. After being attacked, I was determined never to be taken again, never to show weakness again, and especially never to be fooled again," she said.

He read the message loud and clear. She wouldn't play his games.

"Everything isn't always as it appears to be," he told her.

"What is that supposed to mean?" she asked.

"We all have our pasts, and we all have our secrets."

"I'm sure your secrets are about the maid forgetting to pack your lunch," she said, instantly putting her armor into place.

He looked at her, sadness filling him. Did he really seem so cold? "What made you close the doors to Relinquish then?"

She paused for a moment before speaking. "My sister died. I no longer needed to make as much money and I wanted to finally live my dreams."

"I'm sorry…"

"Don't. I can't stand generic apologies, or words that mean nothing. They are spoken so freely, so easily, and they are never meant." She turned away again, and Byron knew he needed to think.

He turned and began walking toward the door.

"Why did you come here? Why did you ask this of me? Is it to prove that I'm worthless in your eyes?"

He could see she was close to falling apart. He should go to her, but he had to get his head clear. This was all too much. He'd learned too much today.

He turned back around. "I'm glad you told me, McKenzie. Sometimes you just have to trust." How ironic that those words were coming from *his* lips. What a crock. He trusted no one, and he hadn't for years.

"It's fine, Byron. Go ahead and leave," she told him.

Pain sliced through him at her words, but that's what he was doing wasn't it? He was leaving. It's what he did best.

Without another word, he slipped from her house. He'd made choices his entire life that affected him — and not in a good way. What was one more bad choice?

CHAPTER THIRTY-ONE

MCKENZIE WAITED UNTIL she was sure Byron was gone, and then she broke down. Everything inside her hurt. She had warned herself not to fall for this man, but she'd gone ahead and done it anyway.

Why? Would she never learn? How could she care about such a cold man? Just because he'd shown her a few glimpses of a real person beneath all that armor, it didn't make him honorable, didn't make him worthy of her love. Maybe that was just it. Maybe she would never find herself worthy to love and so it was easier to love a man who could never possibly love her.

She just had to remember that this was simply one more roadblock on a road with many roadblocks. It wouldn't hold her back forever. She just had to take another detour.

When she went to bed that night, no more tears fell, but not much sleep came either. Her life wouldn't ever be simple, but then who wanted a boring life? It was better to have ups and downs than to just exist.

She'd get past this. She just had to be strong. And she would be.

So when she walked into her office and found Byron there instead of Zach, she wasn't in the most receptive of moods.

"How did you get in here?" was her only question.

"Zach let me in and then split. I think the man might have a slight crush on you, by the way," he said as if he found it amusing.

"Is it such a shock that a man might find me attractive?" she asked as she stood three feet away from him. Enough was enough. They could have it out and then be done with each other.

"I would find it more shocking if men weren't attracted to you," he offered with a laugh.

"I don't find you very funny, Byron. Why don't you tell me whatever it is that you need to say and then get the hell out of my office and out of my life?" Her bravery was going to last only so long before she snapped.

"Fine. Just like that?" he asked. "You want me to just blurt it out?"

"I don't say what I don't mean," she grated out.

"I'm in love with you, McKenzie Beaumont. I can't sleep anymore without you next to me. I can't get you out of my thoughts. I can't function like a normal human being. I've. Fallen. In. Love. With. You."

This made no sense. Although McKenzie thought he had just told her he was in love with her, he was almost yelling at her. The words and the tone didn't match at all.

"In love with me?" she finally asked, her voice low, as if afraid of spooking him. "Did you say that you're in love with me?"

"Before you retreat, or run away, or whatever it is you do when you're getting too close to someone, let me finish. We both spook easily. We both have trust issues. But I know you care about me. I can see it in your eyes, and I can feel it in your touch, in the way you make love to me. I know we have something and I think we would be fools to throw it all away because we're scared."

He began pacing, not looking at her as he delivered his speech. She didn't know what to say, how to respond to him. Not that he was giving her a chance to talk. Right when she opened her mouth to say something, he started speaking again.

"I know I can be blunt, that I come across cold. But I feel different when I'm with you. I want to laugh, to smile, I want to lie beneath the stars and stay there until we've counted them all. I want to give you the stars…" He ran his hands through his hair as he spun back around and then moved toward her, determination in his every step.

"Byron…" She tried to speak again, but he reached her and cupped her face with his hand.

"I won't be my father. I won't cheat or lie, or abuse. I won't be like my mother. They were terrible to each other and they turned something that's supposed to be beautiful into hate and ugliness. I thought that if I felt love, I would behave like they did. But love is a choice, and I choose to love you."

Tears choked her as she looked into his eyes and saw the love shining in them. It was the first time she'd seen such strong emotion on his handsome face, and she couldn't speak past the lump in her throat, so instead of trying to talk right then, she wrapped her arms around him, took his lips with hers, and tried to show him how she felt.

He grabbed her, deepening the kiss for several long heartbeats before he drew back, a mixture of passion and adoration burning in his gaze. It was more than she'd ever hoped to see.

"Don't distract me, woman. I need to know how you feel," he said, though he didn't release his grasp on her.

"I love you, too," she told him. "I never thought I could love anyone. I thought I'd locked that part of me away from the world, and then you stormed in and messed up my so-called perfect life." Her voice broke.

"I don't want to mess up your life. That's not how this is supposed to go, McKenzie."

"Don't worry. Don't worry at all. My life was terrible. I just didn't see it until I met you. I didn't realize that I was living in a world of beige when just around the corner there were exquisite colors waiting for me to discover. You make me feel emotions I've never felt before — good emotions — and I don't want to let that go. I don't want to live my life in fear, or even worse, live my life without any emotions at all."

"Then we will grow together, McKenzie. We will learn how to trust and how to love to the fullest," he promised her. "And we'll do it in each others arms."

"I will take you up on that, Byron Knight."

McKenzie gasped when Byron lifted her into his arms. "What are you doing?"

"We're going to celebrate somewhere a lot more private than this," he said, carrying her down the hall and out of the building.

"Mmm, then hurry…"

She kissed his neck as he rushed to his car. After setting

her inside, he circled around quickly, jumped into the driver's seat, and he pulled her back to him.

"As long as you never stop doing that, Byron, I'll be a very happy woman."

"I can only promise forever," he told her.

And forever is all that she would ask.

EPILOGUE

"COME BACK TO my bed," Tyler said, reaching for her.

Elena turned and smiled. "Do you want me, Tyler?" she asked, moving a little closer.

"You know I do, baby," he said, a smile in place as he threw off the blanket, showing her how much he wanted her with his thick arousal waiting.

"Good. Are you hurting?" she asked, giving him her most seductive smile.

"Oh yeah, baby. I'm hurting," he said, his tongue coming out and wetting his lips.

"Good. Then you're exactly where I want you to be," she said.

He froze, his smile slowly fading at the change in her tone. Her friskiness was gone, and in its place all the hatred she could show was being directed at him.

"What in the world is going on?" Tyler asked.

"Are you confused?" she asked, enjoying her little game.

"Yeah, just a little," he told her as he sat up, pulling

the blanket back over him. That was too bad. She'd been enjoying the view.

"You see, Tyler, I know exactly who you are. You're a spoiled, self-righteous little rich boy who thinks he can have anything he wants. Now, that I've got you all worked up, you can think about the fact that sometimes, you don't get everything you want."

Turning around, Elena smiled in victory. When she'd vowed to take Byron Knight down, she hadn't realized how easy it would be. Men like him should pay, though they rarely did.

This time though, this time, he didn't get what he wanted. She stepped into the bathroom and almost had the door shut when it was thrust back open. Standing there, looking far from pleased was Tyler in all his naked glory.

"Don't even think for one second that you are going to make a comment like that and then just walk away," he said as he took a menacing step toward her.

Elena's heart lodged in her throat. This game had just taken a direction she hadn't been planning on.

If you enjoyed this story, please enjoy a preview of :

UNEXPECTED TREASURE

by Melody Anne

PROLOGUE

"I CAN'T BELIEVE the way the grandchildren are growing like weeds. Little Jasmine is already fifteen, and boy, is she a beauty," Joseph said.

Sitting on the back deck with the morning sun streaming down upon them, Joseph and his brother George were enjoying light breakfast pastries and coffee while catching up on news about the kids and their week.

"I know, Brother. Little Molly is ten years old now. It feels like it was only yesterday that Trenton was fighting tooth and nail not to get married and settle down, and now he and Jennifer have a beautiful family with two kids. Not to mention their rowdy dog, Scooter, and feisty cat, Ginger."

"Don't forget that dang goose. Last time I was there, the rascal got me right in the tush. I need to take my hunting rifle with me the next time that I visit," Joseph threatened.

"If you'd just bring him some cracked corn like I do, he wouldn't chase after you," George said, not even attempting to hide his amusement.

"I'm not bribing a damn bird, and I'm certainly not running from one!"

"Ah, simmer down, Brother. I have a feeling the goose won't be the *end* of you — it's not as if you have a fundamental problem here, and you haven't hit bottom. So forget that cheeky critter and put the incident *behind* you" he guffawed, gleeful at making Joseph the butt of his joke. He tended to go a lot over the top when he found something so amusing.

Joseph mumbled something very unbrotherly under his breath, but he let go of his wrath against both George and the animals at his nephew's home. He had far more important issues to discuss, such as what they were going to eat that night.

"What are the plans for today?" George asked. "With Katherine and Esther out shopping, we can sneak away. I'm sick of golfing. Why don't we race go-karts again? That was a thrill."

"I think you're trying to kill me off, George. You slammed me against the wall the last time we went," Joseph huffed.

"You're acting like an old man, Joseph. We still have lots of life left in these old bones."

"True, George, very true. Fine. I'll give go-kart racing another try, though I hope that these old bones don't become these old *broken* bones. Let's see how many of the grandchildren we can gather up to go with us."

The men continued their morning meal as George pulled out the newspaper and flipped to the business section. Though George's son Trenton was now in charge of Anderson and Sons Incorporated, George still liked to keep up on what was going on in the Seattle area.

Joseph looked up just in time to see George gasp for air, his face white. Frozen with fear for a few endless seconds, Joseph felt his legs finally start working again and he jumped up to help his brother.

"George! What's wrong? Are you choking? Is it your heart? Speak to me, Brother," he urged as he leaned over to see what he could do. They'd had enough health scares to last them a lifetime and Joseph didn't think he could handle another near-death experience in his beloved family.

Just as Joseph began moving to race for the phone, George gestured wildly at the newspaper. Joseph stopped in his tracks and read the largest headline and subheadline on the page: "Billionaire buys flailing computer tech firm: Richard Storm sells East Coast shipping business, brings thousands of jobs to Seattle."

It wasn't the article that had Joseph turning as white as his brother. It was the photograph of a man who appeared to be their age — and who looked almost identical to the two of them, just a different hairstyle, some added wrinkles around the eyes, and a short beard covering his face.

"What is this?" Joseph gasped as he sank down in the chair next to George.

"I don't know. The picture just startled me — that's all. I'm sure it's nothing." George tried to reason it away, but he couldn't stop staring at the still eyes of the man gazing into the camera. It was like looking into a mirror.

"Well, read the dang thing," Joseph nearly shouted as he regained his voice. He pointed to a paragraph in the middle of the first column.

"Storm, who was born in Seattle, moved to the East

Coast with his adoptive parents when still a baby. He says he owes his hard-work ethic to his father, who was a doctor in Seattle for 25 years before moving his medical practice to Portland, Maine. Storm was orphaned at age 18, when his parents died in a boating accident, and he used his modest inheritance to become a shipper of historic relics, mainly hard-to-find European artifacts from the 15th century. By the time he turned 30" — the newspaper gave a date — "he was worth more than $10 million — almost $60 million in today's dollars — and he continued to increase his fortune dramatically. Storm is a now a billionaire several times over."

"He was born here on the same day as we were? This can't be a coincidence."

"Let me keep reading."

"Go on then," Joseph said, still looking at the picture.

"Apparently, he married young, had five children — four boys and one girl — and then their mother left them. He's made the move here because he feels it's the right thing to do for his family."

"We need answers, and I want them now, George."

"I couldn't agree more."

The two men went inside to Joseph's large den and looked through the bookcase containing old family albums. When they came upon the album from the year they were born, they sat with it in front of the fireplace.

Less than an hour later, both men were speechless with shock. Richard Storm's adoptive father was the same man who'd delivered Joseph and George. Their mother even had notes in the album about her doctor, saying how kind he was and how sad she felt that he and his wife were unable to have children.

Only one conclusion appeared likely. This doctor must have seized the opportunity to give his wife a child, too desperate to care about the consequences of ripping another family apart.

"This man, Richard, may very well be our brother," George gasped as he gazed at the pictures of their mother holding them for the first time.

"But how is it possible she had a third child without realizing it?" Joseph countered.

"You know how different times were back then, Joseph. They didn't have ultrasounds, and Mother suffered complications during delivery. She'd lost a lot of blood and they had to put her under. Dad wasn't in the room — back then, fathers didn't belong there. The only other person in the room with the doctor was his nurse, who also happened to be his wife. They could have easily seen the third child and taken the opportunity to create their own family. Why else would they have moved away so suddenly?"

"I just can't imagine that happening."

"That's because, if this is true, we have a brother out there we've missed knowing, and our mother has a child she never knew," George said, overtaken by sadness.

"One thing I know for sure — we need to meet this man and find out if he really is family."

"But what do you think that will do to him, Joseph? We would cause upheaval in his life, change everything that he believes about himself and his loved ones," George said. "Let's try to be reasonable."

"Can you honestly do nothing but stand by when a man who may be our kin is so close by? He has children, George, and they are most likely our nephews and our niece. We have to find out the truth, even if it's a painful one."

"You're right, Joseph. Of course you're right. I just don't know whether our visit will be a welcome one to this man. Heck, we know nothing about him. What if the man who could be our brother is a terrible person?"

"He can't be terrible, George. No matter what his birth certificate says, he's an Anderson, and Andersons are good people," Joseph said with confidence.

"Right you are, Joseph. Well, you know what this means, don't you?"

"Of course I do. Go-kart racing is off the schedule today. It looks like it's time to pay a visit to Richard Storm."

"I'll grab my hat. You lead the way brother; I'm right behind you."

The two men walked out the door, climbed into Joseph's Mercedes and made their way to the new Storm Corporate offices. Expectant smiles spread across their faces as they neared their destination. Granted, it would be heartbreaking to learn they had a brother they hadn't had the pleasure of growing up with. But still, if it were true, they were now blessed with a whole line of family members to get to know.

Joseph grinned, thinking of all those first-rate great-nieces and -nephews. More and more babies on the horizon and potential love matches to make.

CHAPTER ONE

Two years earlier

D O ANY OF you have any idea of what this is about?"

"Not a clue. It seems the old man has got something up his keister again. I haven't gone to bed yet from yesterday. I seriously considered not showing up."

"You may as well stop complaining about it, because you know how father gets. You don't want your precious trust fund cut off, now, do you?"

"Shut up, Brielle. You're the one who'd be hurting if you lost Daddy's money."

"All of you should shut up before the old man walks in. The more compliant we are, the sooner our family reunion can end, and the quicker we can get on with our lives."

"That's very good thinking, Lance. I know how important it is for you to run from my presence."

The five young bickerers turned in surprise to find

their father standing in the doorway. Richard had to quickly disguise the sadness in his eyes. This wasn't the time to coddle his children, who, though grown up, were thoroughly spoiled. It was time to do what he should have done years ago, before it was almost too late. He didn't have much time left, and he feared that his kids would never change if he didn't act now.

Would they even care that the doctor had given him the grim diagnosis of only three years to live? At this point, he doubted they would. It saddened him to no end how much he had failed them — and he was certain that his failures as a parent had caused the distance among them all.

"Fine, you heard us complaining. We're sorry, Dad, but we haven't all been together in one room in years, so what's the big emergency?" Richard watched as his youngest child, Brielle, walked to the liquor cabinet and poured herself a scotch. She was only twenty-four years old, but she had so much bitterness inside her.

Why shouldn't she? Their mother had walked out on all of them, but Brielle was the only one who couldn't remember her — she'd only been three at the time. It made her feel as if she'd really missed out the most. Lance had vague memories, as he had been five, but Tanner, Ashton and Crew remembered the most. The kids were all two years apart, his ex-wife having produced them almost on a strict schedule.

Soon after Brielle was born, Suzanne was done being a mother and left them without ever turning back around. Richard had been too busy for years to date another woman, and when he'd tried, it had always been disastrous, since he'd been too exhausted to put forth any real effort. Eventually, he'd just given up.

He'd been wealthy and worked long hours to become even richer, leaving the children with nannies during the day. Yet he'd felt guilty enough to stay home in the evenings and on the weekends so he could spend as much time as possible with his offspring.

It was only when they'd gotten older that he'd started working even longer hours, and that's when they'd begun to drift away from him. He just hoped it wasn't too late to reverse the damage.

Now, here he stood in a room with grown children ranging in ages from twenty-four to thirty-two, and he didn't like them. He loved them, as he always would, but they'd become selfish and spoiled, and even worse — entitled.

"You've all been cut out of my will and I'm freezing your trust funds."

Richard watched as, slowly, each of his children turned toward him with varying expressions of disbelief. Of course it was Crew who finally cleared all expression from his face as he stood taller and faced his father.

"Do you care to elaborate?"

"My parents were hard workers their entire lives. They built not only one medical practice, but two. They scrimped and saved, and gave me a good education. When they passed, I was devastated, but I took my inheritance and I created something both of them would be proud of. Unfortunately, I've pampered and indulged the five of you, making you think that life is nothing more than one big party, and that you deserve to be handed everything on a silver platter. Well, that stops today. As I've just said, you've been cut out of my will. Your trust funds are frozen, and your credit cards canceled —"

"You can't do that!" Ashton shouted.

"I can and I have. You can leave the room now and be on your way, or you can hear me out."

None of them budged, and Richard made sure to look each child in the eye. He refused to back down this time, no matter how many tears Brielle shed, or how convincing the group charmer, Tanner, tried to be. He would lose his children forever if he didn't stand firm and show them that life was about so much more than what they'd made it.

"You haven't really given us a choice other than to listen to you, have you? Is this your way of saying you need some attention? You could have just scheduled a lunch date," Lance said, trying to make a joke, but the anxiety in the room allowed no break in the tension.

"You always have a choice, Lance. It's your decision whether to make the right one or not. I'm really sorry you feel that way, though. It honestly breaks my heart. We were once a tight-knit family, laughing together, speaking often, *living* our lives. I don't know where I went wrong, but somewhere along the way, you got lost, and now I'm allowing you to find yourselves again. I hope you do."

"OK, OK," Brielle said with a roll to her eyes. "What is this journey you want us to take?"

"I'm glad you asked, Peaches," he replied, reverting to the nickname he'd given her at birth because of the sun-kissed color of her hair, which was as stunning as the beginning rays of a sunset. Her deep-blue eyes widened at the use of the name he and her brothers had always called her. Somehow along the way they had stopped.

Brielle pulled herself together and looked back at her father with rage evident in her now-narrowed eyes. "I haven't been *Peaches* in fifteen years, Dad, but if you want to reminisce about the 'good' old days, then I'll go ahead and play your game."

The sarcasm and scorn pierced Richard to the heart.

"I've sold the family business. I've decided it's time for a fresh start, and I've chosen to do it on the West Coast. There is nothing in Maine to hold me any longer, and I'm tired of the tourist season. I've just finalized the paperwork on a failing computer tech firm, and I plan to turn it around. Doing that gave me an idea for the five of you."

Richard waited for it to sink in that his shipping empire was now gone. He knew Lance would be the most upset, as he'd been the one who'd invested the most time in the corporate offices. Richard missed those days when Lance, still in high school, was eager to learn all he could by his father's side.

Once the boy had left for college, then graduated, that interest had waned, and he acted as if he were just waiting to take over the business, but no longer eager to put in the effort. In the last several years, he'd become as spoiled as his siblings, but Richard, looking forward to a comfortable retirement, had still entertained a hope that the boy would one day take the reins. Now, that wasn't going to happen for his youngest son.

"Can this be reversed?" Lance's voice was strained with the amount of control he had to exert to keep his temper.

"No." Richard didn't elaborate.

"The business was supposed to be mine."

"Then you should have taken pride in it. You should have proved to me that you deserved a stake in the family business. I had hoped to pass it to you one day, but as of right now, you are unworthy to take the reins of any business of mine."

Another son broke in. "Don't you think that's a bit harsh, Father?"

"No, I don't, Crew. And you are no different from your brother. None of you has worked for an honest dollar, and I would rather see my funds passed down to people who can appreciate them than leave them to you with the way you've been acting. You have time to figure this out — well, time for now, at least."

"What is that supposed to mean — *for now*?" Tanner asked.

Richard took a calming breath. It wasn't yet time to tell his children of his prostate cancer. The doctor said he'd done all he could do. Of course, they would keep trying, but his doctor was also a good friend, and he'd warned Richard to get his affairs in order with his grim prognosis. *Three years.*

"Nothing, Tanner. You just need to pay attention. I want you to prove yourselves, make something of your lives. You are more than these spoiled brats I see before me right now."

"How are we supposed to do anything if we have no money? What do you want us to do to *prove* ourselves?" Tanner asked, throwing his hands into the air in exasperation.

"That's the smartest question you've asked me so far," Richard said with a smile before pausing to gaze at each one of his children. A glimmer of hope filled him at the fighting spirit he saw in each of them. "I have purchased five more failing businesses. You can fight amongst yourselves to choose which one you want to run. I have created a sufficient budget for you to do what needs to be done to bring the companies back into profitability. If you do this, and do it well, only then will I reinstate your inheritance. If you fail, you will be on your own."

"Well, what if your idea of a successful business is different from what our idea would be?" Ashton asked.

"When you truly feel success for the first time in your life, you will know what it is. You've never earned that badge of honor before. You'll learn now, one way or the other. I'm done explaining this. You may come see me when you're ready."

Setting down the folders of the five businesses he'd purchased, he noticed that none of the kids jumped up to see what the choices were. He knew they would, though. On the off chance they didn't, it would break his heart, but he would stay true to his word and cut them off. They would either make it, or not. What their decision would be was now out of their hands.

Richard walked from the room, his children bolting after him, trying to chase him down. Though he hadn't let them see the burden weighing on his shoulders, the conversation had hurt him in ways he couldn't begin to describe. He knew he was taking a huge gamble, but what other option had there been?

If he didn't kick his children out of their nest eggs, they'd never learn how to fly, never take pride in a true victory. He could end up losing them forever, but he already felt as if they were so incredibly self-absorbed that their only connection with their family was through blood. Richard had faith that his children would soon find their wings — they'd find their way back to him — and to each other. Only then would he be able to rest in peace.

Closing the door to his study in his children's faces, he

looked down at the framed picture of his parents sitting in its special place on his desk. His mother's eyes were filled with joy as she cuddled him close to her heart. He was only six months old at the time, and it had taken his parents so long to have him that they'd doted on him his entire life.

Still, they'd taught him the core values that made him who he was today. He'd always worked hard, earned everything he'd ever striven for and appreciated the life he'd been raised to lead. He'd gotten lazy with his own children, but he knew it wouldn't be too late. He just had to have faith and stick with the plan.

They would all take it one day at a time, and then a week at a time. If he tried to think past that, it became too overwhelming. He had always protected his children, which he was still doing, just in a more *tough love* sort of way. He was determined that they *would* appreciate this, and him, someday.

Richard smiled as he thought back to their priceless expressions of rage and shock. They wouldn't be appreciating him anytime soon; that was for certain.

Unexpected Treasure is available
at all major retailers.

70949912R00151

Made in the USA
Columbia, SC
18 May 2017